## Cold Christmas

Josephine's head sank low upon her pillow and her eyes closed despite themselves. She came back to full consciousness with a jerk. Again, she saw the little dark girl in her room. She was standing with her back to the window, looking at Josephine and smiling shyly.

'Hullo!' said Josephine, a little startled. 'I never saw you come in. Do you want anything? What is your name?'

The child did not reply. Josephine's eyes flicked back to her book for a moment and when she looked again the little girl was gone.

*Also by Nina Beachcroft*

A Spell of Sleep
Under the Enchanter
A Visit to Folly Castle
Well Met by Witchlight

# Nina Beachcroft

# COLD CHRISTMAS

MAMMOTH

First published in Great Britain 1974
by William Heinemann Ltd
Published 1991 by Mammoth
an imprint of Mandarin Paperbacks
Michelin House, 81 Fulham Road, London SW3 6RB

Mandarin is an imprint of the Octopus Publishing Group,
a division of Reed International Books Ltd

ISBN 0 7497 0726 7

A CIP catalogue record for this title
is available from the British Library

Printed in Great Britain
by Cox and Wyman Ltd, Reading, Berks.

# I

When Josephine heard that they were going away on Christmas Eve to spend three nights with some people she didn't know, she was aghast. She wrote it in her diary on December 23rd.

'I am aghast.' Aghast meant 'stupefied with horror', and that described her emotions very well. She was aghast mainly because Christmas would be all wrong now: they would not be having Granny and Aunt Ruth to lunch on Christmas Day; they would not be going to them on Boxing Day, and these things they had done ever since Josephine could remember. Her parents were the kind of parents who always did the same thing every year in a predictable way, so Josephine was all the more amazed that this year they had broken with tradition.

'But of course,' she thought, stiffening all over with shyness and depression as she and her parents got out of the car with their suitcases and the present (a pink potted plant) they were giving to their host and hostess: 'everything has gone wrong since Daddy lost his job.' Her father had been made redundant at work two months previously; since then he had been about the house a good deal. He had somehow shrunk and grown a little older in this time too: he was nearly fifty, old for a father with a daughter

Josephine's age and this was worrying as it meant it would be difficult to find another job easily. And Josephine would have to go to a different school ... one for which fees did not have to be paid.

She pushed these thoughts behind her to the back of her mind. She wasn't going to like this Christmas. She could tell from the weary way her father got out of the car that he felt much the same about it as she did. It was all her mother's fault: *she* had fixed up this horrible visit to utter strangers.

'Hullo there.' Their hostess came to greet them wearing a yellow polo-necked jersey and an old pair of trousers. She was much younger than Josephine's mother, unmade up, with a bony, horsy face and a lot of fair hair down her back. Two or three children of different shapes and sizes appeared in the large hall of the house behind her, dressed also in old jerseys and trousers. Josephine, carefully organized by her mother into her best wool frock and white nylon tights, felt instantly over-dressed and wrong. One of the children, a girl some three years younger than Josephine with an unbrushed thicket of reddish hair, came further out into the hall and stared at Josephine in an unpleasant way. Josephine turned her back on her.

'You haven't met my husband and daughter yet, have you Tessa?' her mother was saying. 'It really is very good of you to invite us all over like this. Don, this is Tessa Swift. And I hardly need introduce you to Tony Swift; we feel we know him already, having seen him every Friday night for so many weeks.'

'Don't hide, Tony,' his wife said, opening a door that gave onto the hall and calling her husband. 'Guests. Here are Don and Rita Palmer and Josephine.'

'How do you do?'

More introductions all round. Josephine was very careful

not to be impressed by Mr Anthony Swift who was a television actor and had been appearing as hero in some costume drama or other on Friday evenings. She had only bothered to watch one episode. He didn't look at all young either: if you looked closely there was some grey by his ears and he was fat. Or anyway his stomach bulged out both below and above his belt and his bottom stretched his pale blue corduroy jeans.

'How do you do?' said her father to Anthony Swift so loudly and heartily and unlike his normal self that Josephine knew he was feeling awkward and unwilling and wrong too. But her mother was all smiles and gush. The trouble was that there had ever been the friendship between her mother and this Mrs Swift who must be a good ten years younger and rather a different sort of person. But they had met at an art class and Mrs Swift had much admired Mrs Palmer's water-colours. For they were good, Josephine herself had to admit it. Her mother had even sold a few of them. She specialized in local country views and houses: was looking forward to painting the Swift's house: this chilly mansion of stone pillars and steps and draughty halls. Josephine refused to be impressed by it. 'Our house is much nicer,' she thought loyally, remembering central heating and wall-to-wall carpeting and other comforts they had left behind them. Their poor little house ... shut up and deserted and all alone over Christmas ...

There was a large landing upstairs: more people—boys mostly—came to look over the banisters which curved elegantly up again to another landing above. Josephine gave them one glance, then stared at the floor—slippery it was and squared all over with black and white tiles, like a chessboard.

'Come up and I'll show you your rooms.' Mrs Swift bent to pick up their big suitcase.

'Tony—you might perhaps—' she suggested. But Mr Swift, having said 'how do you do' in a rather snooty conceited manner (Josephine thought) had faded away. So Mrs Swift and Josephine's father, fighting each other politely for possession of the suitcase, struggled together up the stairs.

Josephine and her mother followed. It had been merely chilly in the hall but now an icy breath of air met them upon the stairs. It was very cold weather indeed outside too and as the sun was going, the frost bit deep. There didn't seem much heating in this big old house. It was going to be a cold Christmas and funnily enough, that was the name of the house. Cold Christmas. They were visiting a house called Cold Christmas at Christmas time and it was icy! Although this fitted well artistically, Josephine supposed, she would rather not experience it and she went into her dark high box of a room shivering with reluctance and dismay. It wasn't furnished comfortably either: dark polished floor of ice, little blue mat upon it by little blue bed. Icicle-white thin curtains that moved out into the room propelled by unseen trickles of cold air. A coffin-like wardrobe: dirty frozen-pond colour. An uneasy, tight feeling in Josephine's head. Perhaps it was going to snow.

A cold Christmas indeed.


In the larger room next door Josephine could hear her mother giving the plant in its pot to Mrs Swift. It wasn't the kind of thing one could hide and produce on the proper day: Mrs Swift must have been politely pretending not to notice it all the way up the stairs.

'But how lovely,' Josephine heard her say. 'We'll have it downstairs. I know just the place for it. Come down when you're ready and I'll show you round the place. Did you know I bred donkeys? Josephine might like to see them.'

She descended the stairs. Josephine looked out of her room and saw a clod of earth fall out of the pot onto the hall floor which Mrs Swift did not notice. Josephine felt shy about it: what should she do, should she call out to her? The earth would get kicked about the hall and trodden in if it wasn't noticed. She was sorry her parents had given such a conspicuous and awkward present ... she wished ... she wanted ... Oh, if they could just go back home! In spite of the donkeys.

Mrs Swift had disappeared. An assortment of children still watched her. Josephine retreated from their eyes through the half open door of her parents' room. She could hear giggling and whispering behind her. She shut the door.

Her parents' room was big with twin beds and a large window. Her father was standing by it looking out.

'It must have been a beautiful garden once,' he was saying.

The garden was on the slope of a hill and had been terraced. The top terrace was mainly gravel and old stone urns and bits of broken balustrade, then a flight of steps to lawn and bare-looking flower beds of different shapes, then a holly hedge and another dip down to rough tawny grass and the brown ghosts of dead weeds and more ever-green bushes and the beginning of a long avenue of oaks, mostly very old and half fallen down. To one side of the avenue glimmered a partially iced-over lake, surrounded by bushes and trees and rough pasture land.

'I don't believe they've had the place very long,' said Josephine's mother, joining her husband at the window. 'It will take a lot of money to keep up, although as early Georgian houses go it's not all that big. Did you see how the stucco was falling and being pulled down by the creeper

5

at the front of the house? Someday they'll have to do something about that.'

'I suppose they have lots of money or they wouldn't have bought the place. Successful actors on television must make quite a bit. What's she? She doesn't look the show biz type herself.'

'I think perhaps she has county connections,' replied Josephine's mother vaguely. 'She has a lovely speaking voice anyway, hasn't she? She may well have money behind her.'

'A handsome old house really.' Josephine's father sighed deeply as he said it and hunched his shoulders together.

'I'm sure I'll find something good to sketch and to paint,' said Mrs Palmer, 'though really of course it's only a very minor example of the Palladian style: a pleasant, family house but nothing particularly outstanding about it. I like the big bow windows of the sitting room and bedroom above, and the balustrade at the top, of course. Oh, I ought to be able to get something down on paper. I don't quite know what they've got planned for us to do, if anything. They may be the kind of people who like to play charades or indoor games or something. That might be fun, mightn't it?'

Fun? Josephine and her father exchanged looks of mutual horror. They were alike in some ways, certainly in wishing to be left mainly alone and not to be organized.

'I'm not playing at charades or anything with that ghastly lot,' said Josephine coldly and forbiddingly.

'I think Mrs Swift's older girl must be younger than you,' her mother went on with determination, 'but I saw some boys—I don't think they can be hers, perhaps they are cousins or something—who look about your age.'

Boys: was this supposed to cheer her up?

'They wouldn't want me anyway,' said Josephine stiffly.

6

'It would do you good to mix a little with some boys,' her mother continued relentlessly, 'after your convent school. You'll have to meet lots next term, won't you?'

Josephine winced and her mind shied desperately away from the approaching worry. A new school, comprehensive, with boys as well as girls. Nobody would like her. They might all laugh at her because she had been to a private school. She couldn't bear to think of it. It was three years since she had been to a school with boys in it. She didn't want to have anything to do with such creatures.

'I wonder whether we hadn't better go downstairs and brave the merry throng,' said her father at this point, taking Josephine's hand.

So they went out onto the landing and as they did so Josephine noticed a little girl slip out of her room and run away.

'Looking at my things,' she thought. 'What cheek! She must be another cousin, not one of *their* children as she's dark and not all red tangled curls. Where has everybody else gone then? They seem to have deserted us.'

And so Josephine and her mother and father went down the wide flight of stairs into the hall and wondered what to do and where to go next. The earth still lay in a lump in the middle of a white tile. Nobody had noticed it. Josephine carefully averted her eyes. She did not want to feel responsible for it.

'Let's try this door,' said her father bravely.

# 2

Again Josephine stood in the hall outside various closed doors, but this time she was alone. It was some three hours later. She had felt she could not endure to be any longer with Miranda and Annabella, the Swifts' two little girls. In any case, Annabella, who was only four, was now being put to bed by the au pair girl. The boys had disappeared long ago. The only thing for Josephine to do was to find her parents: but the closed door of the sitting room barred the way.

It is sometimes very hard to open a door and go into a room. She could hear voices and laughter and the chink of glasses. When she opened the door and looked in would everybody turn and stare at her? Her hand moved towards the door handle, and fell again in an agony of shyness and self-consciousness. Oh this was a horrid house! She didn't like the black and white hall, the little alcove where a large pot of dried grasses stood, the tall grandfather clock in the corner by the front door which ticked accusingly at her: 'You have no place here, you have no place here. Cold, cold, no comfort, no ease, this is not your sort of house at all, get out, get *out*.'

Poor Josephine might have been a good deal longer in

the hall if there had not come a quick click, click, pitter-pat of feet, busily trotting.

Susie, the large poodle bitch, swung into view from the back regions, the nails of her paws clicking on the floor. She wagged her tail amiably at Josephine and scratched in a purposeful manner at the sitting room door. 'They had better let *me* in, and quickly,' appeared to be her attitude.

So Josephine at last opened the door and sidled in behind the dog, rather wishing she had her complete self-assurance.

In fact of course it was perfectly all right except that there did seem to be a great and confusing number of people in the room. At last she saw Mrs Swift standing by the high white mantelpiece, in front of a log fire; she had changed into a long skirt and her hair was twisted into a knot at the back.

'Hullo,' she called vaguely to Josephine. Then Josephine spotted her parents sitting side by side on a huge white sofa, and went over thankfully towards them. There was a grand piano at one end of the room with a number of photographs and a big jug of white chrysanthemums on it. There were long dark blue curtains at the windows, and a huge Christmas tree, and then she was able to see with some relief that one of the boys was there; the amiable, rather plump one called Jason. He too had a parent present; he must be the son of the little talkative man who produced Anthony Swift's television series.

But there were a lot of other people, two or three very arty and got-up looking girls in their twenties, two or three young men, a couple of smart middle-aged women, all moving about the room with drinks in their hands and talking. None of them took any notice of Josephine at all, which was a great relief.

'Come on, Jason,' Anthony Swift was saying in a teasing voice. 'Tell us nicely in front of the company then, we all appreciate a good limerick,' and Jason was smiling and squirming, rather pink in the face and obviously not wanting to tell whatever limerick it was.

'No, really, Tony, it's rather too rude,' he was saying, and then Josephine's father kindly and tactfully attracted Tony Swift's attention by saying suddenly, in a loud voice, 'Tell me, why is your house called Cold Christmas? It's such an unusual name, isn't it? Is there some story behind it?'

'Not that we know of,' called Tessa Swift, moving over to the sofa. 'It's been very hard for me to discover much about it at all, the house has changed hands so many times. And apparently there was another house here before, which fell into a ruin and was pulled down. We think somebody must have owned either of the houses or the land round about, who was called Christmas, or Christian, or even Christy, and the cold part could have come later. Cold is used in other place names in the county: there are a couple of Coldharbours, which is thought to be a reference to the coldness of the clay, and clay is a cold, heavy soil, of course.'

'Except that this house is built up on the hill, on chalk,' put in Tony Swift, abandoning his teasing of Jason.

'Yes, but it's clay down at the bottom. The house could have been named from the fields round about.'

They went on discussing this and the date the house was built, which was supposed to have been around 1750 or so, and Josephine and Jason caught one another's eyes.

'Did Tessa show you the donkeys?' asked Jason.

'Yes.'

'But I bet she didn't show you everything: the stables and the cows and all.'

'No, just the donkeys. They were sweet.'

'Would you like to see some more, then?'

'Yes, all right.'

They escaped together into the hall, followed by the dog, a willing partner to any enterprise.

'Silly man: I do hate silly show-offs like Tony,' announced Jason as he shepherded Josephine down a passage towards the back premises.

'My father says he's not even a good actor but he has charisma and so they've got to have him.'

'He has *what*?' asked Josephine.

'Oh—I don't know what it means actually but people seem to like him and that's what counts I suppose. *I* prefer Tessa, don't you?'

'I don't really know them yet,' replied Josephine carefully. 'She seems quite nice. I don't know really why she's asked us except that Mummy is going to paint their house.'

'Oh Tessa's very hospitable you see,' said Jason. 'She makes up for Tony who doesn't really like people very much, though he likes to *seem* to be hospitable. Do you get what I mean?'

'Well—sort of.'

'It's more than I do. Wow! It's cold outside!'

He opened a door into the stable yard at the back of the house: a sword of ice leapt down their throats: the stone yard glittered and sparkled with frost. A sharp banging crack of hoof against wood came from within a stable door and the pulling sound of a rope through an iron ring.

'A horse,' said Jason, waving his hand towards the stable. 'I don't like them, myself. But you might want to see?'

'Oh *yes*.'

'Funny. I like showing people round,' he said, inverting his upper half slowly over a waist-high railing until his head touched the ground beneath, then up again. 'It's not even my place and I've only been here once before. Last Christmas. Just after they bought this place. You see my father's known Tony for years. I don't live anywhere like this myself : just a flat in London with my Mum and my elder brother. He's in Africa now. I miss him rather. My father has me for holidays sometimes. My parents are divorced.'

'Oh,' said Josephine, dragging herself back from ecstatic communion with a beautiful bay gelding. 'What about the other boys? I thought you were all brothers or cousins or something. You seemed to know each other so well.'

'We met last year—and Simon and I go to the same school. He's a cousin to the other two, Rob and Rupert, who are brothers. They're all Tessa's relatives. Simon's mother was going to be here but she had to spend Christmas with some sick old auntie or something. The others often come on their own; their parents are abroad. They are a beastly lot of kids, really.'

'What—Simon and Rupert and Rob, *all* of them beastly?' said Josephine absently as she reached out a hand towards a dappled grey pony.

'Yes. Simon's the worst. He's the end. I know because I'm at school with him. The others are planning to do something about Simon.'

'What?'

'I don't know yet. Wow! Fell off!'

Showing off slightly but nevertheless engaging, Jason picked himself up from a pile of straw. He had been trying to walk along the low top of a stall partition.

'Never could balance very well,' he said cheerfully.

'Where shall we go now?'

'*I* don't know. Thought you might have an idea ... Behind this side of the stables as you see is the field with the donks in and then—oh, opposite's the cows. Tessa has two Jersey cows. Last year it was ducks. Some on the lake and some in a stable up here. Don't ask me why.'

'What, you mean she keeps cows in the stalls over the yard there? Oh do let's see.'

'Surely. They're called Daisy and Primrose. The names are up over the stalls. Oh no, they aren't. Well, they ought to be. If *I* had cows I'd put up their names, wouldn't you?'

'Oh *yes*,' replied Josephine enthusiastically, drowning now in the extreme cow-ness of cows. They were so soft, so gentle, had such big eyes with such pale lashes, such daft faces, such sweet-hay breath ...

She retreated a little from the sweet-hay breath.

'Ooh, she let me stroke her nose.'

'Oh, I daresay,' said Jason, a little bored now, but graciously condescending to her girlish pleasure. 'Shall we go into the kitchen? We might hurry up those Spaniards with our supper—we're having a supper apart from the grown-ups in the billiard room.'

'Oh. Good.'

For the first time that day Josephine smiled, a broad smile which lit up her pale, rather thin face and made it look almost pretty. She felt internally too as if a lump of something hard within her was beginning to melt.

Within the kitchen there was another crowd of people. The first familiar figure Josephine noticed was the dog who had long ago tired of their cold exploration of the stable yard and retreated inside in search of her dinner bowl.

The two dark Spaniards, the woman in an apron, the man in a white coat, were loading food onto plates and trollies, helped by Mrs Swift and the Swedish au pair girl. Mrs Swift looked like the Swedish girl might do in ten years time if she had been left out in a lot of wind and rain, thought Josephine, not altogether kindly. But Tessa Swift's rather weatherbeaten look had its own attraction: she looked athletic and healthy. In and out of everybody's feet ran Miranda, the older of the two Swift girls who had evidently successfully resisted attempts to make her go to bed.

'We must have candles!' she was shouting. 'Candles! Just like you in the dining room!'

'Just wait a moment, Miranda, until I've finished what I'm doing,' said her mother.

'But I want them *now*. Green ones to go with the room. Mumm*ee*. You know we've got some somewhere. Oh where are they?'

And Miranda in an excited, wrought-up way began pulling at drawer after drawer in the kitchen dresser.

'*No*, Miranda, do wait, please. Oh Greta, Greta, do be a lamb and find whatever the wretched child wants. Jason, would you like to ring the gong? Not too loudly, but it'll let everybody know that their supper's ready. *No Miranda*, you can't ring the gong. Jason will do it properly and not bang the wall behind it.'

'No, indeed—' Jason looked important and strode off towards the hall, pursued by Miranda. A strange pandemonium presently arose out of which one could detect both the mature and practised hand of Jason doing his careful best '*boom* boom *boom* boom', and then a wild crescendo which evidently meant that Miranda had wrung the baton from his hand and was doing her worst.

'Josephine, here are the candles. I've just found them and some candlesticks, if you and Greta would like to light them and put them round your table that would be a great help.'

Mrs Swift went off with a tray of glasses, ignoring her daughter, now quite out of control on the gong, who was however suddenly caught up from behind by her father and given two resounding smacks on her bottom.

'Ow!' She was preparing to yell but caught Josephine's eye and followed her into the billiard room, muttering nothing more than, 'You'll have to let me light the candles then.'

The billiard room was long and had white panelling. It was difficult to see if they were eating off the billiard table or not as it was covered entirely with a white table-cloth. At one end of the table the Swedish girl Greta, looking rather flushed, was ladling out a pot of what looked like chicken stew. There were hot rolls, too.

'I'm going to sit at the head of the table and Rob can be at the foot,' announced Miranda, when all the candles were alight. 'I've chosen Rob because I don't like you to-night, Jason.'

'Couldn't care less.'

The others found their seats as best they could. Greta finished serving them and then heaped a big plate for herself, saying:

'Your mother told me to sit and eat with you and watch how you behave but I am too exhausted and so I go to my room, you can tell her, if she desires to know.'

'Goodnight, Greta Garbo,' called Rob with a daring and rather rude whistle after her as she closed the door, while his younger brother, Rupert, giggled and flicked a bit of bread at Miranda.

''Ere 'ere, order.' Jason rapped the table with his knife vainly and Josephine's heart sank. She wished Greta had stayed: she really did not want this meal to degenerate into a bread fight. She began to eat her stew very fast, casting sidelong looks at Simon who sat opposite her and who had not spoken at all. What had Jason meant when he had said Simon was the end? Perhaps he had misjudged

Simon and Simon was really very nice, and unjustly persecuted by the others. Rob and Rupert were evidently loud-mouthed rowdies: they looked it anyway. They both had cheerful, thick-lipped rather coarse faces with thick, tough bodies and very scuffed shoes. They looked as if they could both take and give a good deal of punishment. It was not long before Rupert and Miranda were locked in mortal combat under the table.

Josephine noticed that Simon, like herself, was eating very quickly. Then, just as Jason and Rob were pulling Rupert back to his chair and telling him to behave himself or they would have the grown-ups about their ears, Simon deliberately leant across the table and blew out all the candles. The central light had been turned off by Greta as she left the room and so they were now in utter darkness.

'What now,' thought Josephine, trying to find her mouth with her hot roll. She sat tight and still in her chair trying to control a creepy feeling about the back of her neck. She really could see nothing.

'Oh *Simon*,' came Jason's voice. 'That's not funny. We'll break something and then there'll be trouble.'

'I'll get the light on,' said Rob. 'No—*ouch*!' There was a thump and a scuffle and a call of 'Oh you beast' from somebody and then at last the light went on. It was Rupert who had made his way to it, Rob and Simon were found to be fighting in the centre of the room.

Josephine half got up from her chair and as she did so felt a painful pull from behind: she could not raise her head.

'Oh!' she cried in surprise and pain and found that someone had stolen behind her and tied her plaits to the back of the chair in the dark. That explained the creepy feeling, but what an unkind trick!

Jason helped her free herself. 'It was Simon,' he said.

'I suppose it must have been.' Josephine already felt a good deal less disposed to think of him as a misunderstood character.

'You are an ass, Simon,' cried Rob. 'Do stop mucking about and let's have some pudding. There's a lemon meringue pie on the side. Suppose someone had upset that?'

They began to eat the pie in comparative peace and quiet.

'You looked awfully silly with your plaits tied like that,' said Simon addressing Josephine for the first time. He was a thin, dark, good-looking boy who looked clean and open and as if he could never do wicked deeds by stealth, but his eyes sparkled at her with malice. He was dangerous.

Josephine did not know how to handle him. Her eyes still smarted with tears from the pain and shock, so she said nothing but continued eating pie.

'Oh nose in the air, all niminy piminy,' sang Simon to her. 'Well-brought-up little girl from a convent school.'

'I'm not!' flashed Josephine. How could he know? How could he put his finger with such unerring accuracy on such a sensitive spot?

'I heard your mamma and Tessa talking, that's how. Tessa was thinking of sending Miranda there, to civilize her a little, she said.'

Now he had both the girls furious. But Miranda merely put out her tongue while Josephine sat, speechless. All her fears returned to her: how could she cope if at the school she was going to there was a boy like Simon?

'I'll tell you something,' said Jason at Josephine's elbow. 'Simon and I are at this co-educational boarding school, girls and boys. And I'd choose a *girl* to sit next to at dinner rather than Simon.'

It was rather a backhanded compliment but Josephine appreciated the kindness behind it.

'I'm changing schools anyway,' she managed to mutter. Rob and Rupert now began an argument with Simon and Miranda over the size of their second helpings—so under cover of the noise Josephine was able to ask Jason a casual question which meant a great deal more to her than he could know.

'Tell me, Jason, at your school, do they, the boys I mean, do they tease the girls very much?'

'Oh *no*. We don't notice the girls really much at all. It's different by about the fourth year. But not us lot. We never sit next to the girls at dinner or anything like that. Or in class. So you wouldn't get your plaits tied up if *that's* bothering you. I told you Simon was the end, didn't I?'

'I'm not bothered really at all,' and Josephine thankfully changed the subject.

Eventually the Spanish couple came in and cleared the table. A colour television set was discovered to be at one end of the room and showing a Western film. Slowly the boys disposed themselves about it. Miranda disappeared and then reappeared with a pile of cushions and they all lay on the floor. A great deal more time went by. The Western was succeeded by carol singing. It was hours past bedtime but as Miranda was still downstairs, Josephine's sense of honour would not let her go to bed first, as she was secretly longing to do.

At last a great noise of talking and laughing was heard in the hall.

'Goodness, we'd forgotten all about you children, you've been so quiet. Have you been watching television all the time? It's a quarter to midnight.'

'Since they're up they'd better come out with us, hadn't they?' said Jason's father. 'If the animals are going to speak to us I'm sure the children would like to hear them.'

'*What?*'

'What animals?'

'What are you going to do?'

'Come on chaps and wenches,' said Tony Swift very heartily indeed 'It's Christmas Eve and we—no, it was you, Janey darling wasn't it,' he put his arms round one of the pretty girls. 'Janey says on Christmas Eve on the stroke of midnight if you go into the stables the animals will talk to you, it's an old Austrian folk story isn't it, Janey?'

'Russian, I think,' said Janey.

'It'll be very cold out there,' put in Josephine's mother a little anxiously. 'Josephine, if you're coming you must put on your warm coat—'

Josephine winced away from her mother: she hated being singled out like this.

'We'll all put on warm coats,' cried Tony Swift, who appeared to be the motivating spirit behind this excursion.

And so they did with a great deal of chattering and laughter and confusion and then the front door was opened and they all went outside.

Outside it was a different world.

A world of ice and moonlight: calm and splendid. The gravel and then the grass crunched and crisped as they walked on it. A thousand stars burnt and the moon rode high and full. They passed a great motionless mass of bushes and trees layered in shadow and white light; frozen structures of twig and evergreen leaf and moulded bark that looked as if they had been designed by art rather than nature. The stillness made one want to speak in a whisper.

'You know if animals *could* speak this would be a night on which they would,' said Jason in a low voice at Josephine's elbow.

'Do you—do you think there's anything in it, do you think they possibly could?'

'Na-ow, don't be *soppy*,' cried Rob, suddenly running by with a yell.

Voices were getting much louder again. Even the grown-ups had hushed and quietened when they first went out. The children were a little apart, but they could hear Tony Swift's laugh and a remark from Tessa about not upsetting or exciting her donkeys too much.

'I think Daddy's a bit *drunk*,' said Miranda. 'So's your daddy, Jason.'

'Oh no, I don't think so, not particularly,' said Jason with a knowledgeable air.

'I don't like that silly girl called Janey with the silly laugh,' went on Miranda rather vindictively. 'She's showing off horribly.'

Josephine noticed her parents, walking a little behind the others. They were arm in arm. Something about their separateness from the larger group of adults made her want to go to them. But she did not.

Tessa Swift led the way to the paddock in which the fourteen donkeys had a large shed. A path led through the paddock to the stables and stable yard behind. The donkeys were all together, out of their shed in a group, some lying down, others standing over them with drooping heads. They looked like the ghosts of donkeys and their backs and long ears were rimed with frost. In the bright moon-light it was just possible to see the white cloud their breath made about them. Then Tessa shone her torch over them, and those that were touched by its yellow glare were transformed into ordinary brown and grey furry animals blinking in the light. Josephine had a longing to run her fingers right down the black line along the nearest donkey's back. But she was not near enough.

'Hullo darlings,' called Tessa Swift softly. 'Hullo Albert, hullo Rosina. Follow me then, darlings. No, I haven't any food. Let's let them into the yard, Tony. They can have a little hay. And then we can assemble the animals all together and wait for the stroke of midnight.'

'How long to go?' called the young woman named Janey.

'Another five minutes, I make it.'

'Is the stable clock accurate?'

'Near enough,' said Tony Swift, 'near enough. And it strikes. I warrant you that. Ha! 'Ere the clock strikes I'll despatch another villain yet!'

He pirouetted about, flourishing an imaginary sword and even Josephine had to laugh.

'Daddee! Daddee!' screamed Miranda, accurately sensing that liberties would be allowed. 'Carry me over your shoulder and I'll pretend to be a corpse!'

And so she was slung over her father's shoulder where she at first lay in a convincing enough corpse-like manner and then enlivened her journey by attempting to reach his bottom and beat it with her fists.

At last they were all in the yard, donkeys as well, whose little hooves were clacking on the cobblestones as they roamed about. A wild noise of startled barking suddenly arose from within the kitchen.

'Oh, let Susie out for God's sake, Tessa, or she'll ruin everything.'

So now they had an excited dog running about amongst the donkeys, and Tessa opened the various stable-top-doors and they saw the enquiring heads of the two horses and the pony.

'I don't quite know what to do about Daisy and Primrose,' she said. 'They'd be frightened. I can't let them out.'

A low worried-sounding moo echoed her words.

'Open the door but leave them within their stalls,' suggested her husband. 'If they're frightened they'll stay inside. And if they're moved to speech we're bound to hear.'

'Let's hope that what they say won't be too uncomplimentary,' Josephine heard her father murmur.

'Hark, the witching hour has come,' called somebody.

'Hush—Hush you all.' Tony Swift dominated the scene with an arm stretched dramatically upwards. 'Yea, it strikes.'

And the stable clock true to its cue and rather thinly and wheezily began to strike 'One—two—three—

'—ten—eleven—twelve.'

A pause: a hush, except that the animals were still moving about. One of the horses coughed. Yet all these bodies, human beings and animals, waiting, watching each other seemed to begin to mount up, there was a gathering feeling ...

Then Tony Swift laughed. 'Come on, we're waiting,' he called. 'Utter, you beasts.'

Somebody else said something under their breath and then one of the middle-aged women in furs and smart boots stamped her foot and said she was cold.

'And it's Christmas morning,' she exclaimed. 'Happy Christmas, everyone.'

This broke up everything. Instantly the adult members of the party began moving about, talking and laughing.

'Oh!' Josephine could have cried with frustration. *Just* as something was about to happen ... she was sure ...

She was not the only one to feel like this. Suddenly Miranda precipitated herself at her mother, shrieking at her in rage. 'Stop talking! Stop talking all of you! Oh, why must you spoil everything!'

'You didn't give them a chance,' called another voice which Josephine recognized, rather to her surprise, as

Simon's. 'You *fools*. You were just laughing and not attending. Bloody lot of fools.'

'It may be Christmas morning but it is also bedtime,' came Tony Swift's voice, a good deal less jovially. 'Come on, Miranda, and stop behaving so badly.'

It was no use. Josephine felt as if she must explode. Something—the fact that it was now Christmas Day or that it was after midnight—got into her and Simon. They raced off together with the donkeys who were beginning to crowd back into their paddock; they pushed through the pack of them, making them canter and kick. Then Susie the dog barked and ran after them and Rob and Rupert and Jason also ran, shouting.

'Careful, careful, come back—don't excite the donkeys,' Josephine heard Tessa crying after them and then she and the boys were climbing the fence out onto the drive and the large garden beyond.

'Hide and seek, come on, let's play hide and seek,' cried Rob. 'You can find Rupert and me. Come on, Rupe, I know where to go.'

Smooth grass underfoot, between flower beds, careful, there were very black shadows, then between tall hollies that had once been trimmed but now had grown into strange, out of proportion shapes, down stone steps, just seen in time, to more short grass and a long walk between high hedges: at the end an ornamental pond with a thin sheet of ice over it. Josephine paused here to regain her breath. She was alone, though she could hear receding footsteps and cries.

Oh! if she could only break free—if something could break—if she could understand—if there wasn't always somebody spoiling it all! She didn't altogether know what she felt except that her emotions were pent-up and strong. Gradually she quietened and looked back at the house. It

23

was there—large, imposing, glaring light from many of its windows, at the top of the hill dominating the quiet valley beneath. The country round it was so huge, so calm. There were no other houses or lights in sight. The house was life, change, noise. Out here was peace, silence, eternity. She felt she belonged outside and yet she could not stand it, she wanted to shiver.

And then she looked at the frozen pond and it seemed to her that a great eye within it blinked. She knew she was partly imagining it, a cloud had passed over the moon and darkened it, but then she heard, from somewhere down at the bottom of the garden, a deep, panting noise and a steady thump, thump. It could be horses, galloping. Were they coming closer? *Anything* could come up, out of those black bushes and trees.

She stood still a moment, as frozen as the pond. Then she ran, back towards the house, up the steps, colliding with Jason coming down, across the top lawn to the circle of light thrown by the hall and open front door. People were still coming in and out and here Josephine met her mother.

And so there was nothing to do but go to bed. But some words that Simon had spoken echoed in her ears as her tired legs toiled up the stairs.

'You fools,' he had said. 'You *fools*.'

# 3

It was beginning to get light. Josephine turned over in bed and opened her eyes. She felt something across her feet: yes, they had remembered. Somehow her mother had remembered her stocking and had brought it into her room when she was asleep, just as she did every Christmas.

So that was a good start. She had a new pack of cards, crayons, a notebook, a comic, a puppet mouse that fitted over her finger. Not so bad at all.

She heard footsteps quietly descending the stairs, but apart from that everything was still and silent. When she could bear it no longer, she washed and dressed and went into her parents' room.

'Is that you, Josephine?' called her mother's voice anxiously as she gently turned the door knob. 'Oh, it is, good. Come on in. You can see why I was worried it might be Tessa or the Spanish cook bringing us early morning tea!'

Josephine stared and began to laugh. Her parents really did look very funny because they were both in one of the single beds together and on top they had piled the blankets from the other bed. On top of that was the small woolly rug which had lain on the floor between the two beds.

'I was so cold when I woke up about an hour ago,' said

her mother, 'that this seemed the only solution. Do you know these beds only have two thin blankets and a cotton eiderdown each and there's no heating in the room at all that I can see. I've twisted all the knobs I can find on that radiator by the window but nothing has happened. Tell me darling, were *you* warm enough?'

'After I'd gone to bed in my socks and jersey I was.'

'But I'm *terrified* Tessa will come and find me like this. Perhaps I had better get up instead. She's really so kind though rather vague about comfort and I don't want to hurt her feelings. After all, although she has some help she is working very hard.'

'I don't think she will come in,' said Mr Palmer. 'Don't you remember she said something last night about driving the Spanish couple to Mass early this morning and did anyone else want a lift there, or to the church in the village. I shall walk to the eleven o'clock service by the way, Josephine, if you want to come. Jason and his father will probably be coming too.'

'Yes, all right, Daddy.'

'I wonder what is planned for breakfast if they're all out?' said Mrs Palmer dubiously. 'I forgot to ask what time breakfast was.'

'Golly I'm hungry,' said Josephine looking out of the window. 'Thank you so much for the lovely stocking but I wish you'd put an apple in it! I love the little mouse. I've read the comic and drawn a picture: and what shall we *do* about breakfast? When shall I give you my presents? When will you give me your proper presents? You did manage to bring yours to me down here, didn't you? I know I'm not to expect Granny's, or Aunt Ruth's or godparents' or anything and that they're all waiting at home—but you did bring me your big one from you both, didn't you?'

'Yes, yes. Don't worry. I think there's going to be a kind

of present-giving session this morning before lunch round the Christmas tree. Tell me, Josephine—are you enjoying it here all right now you're getting to know the other children?'

'Not too bad,' admitted Josephine cautiously. 'This place gives me rather a funny feeling though. It's odd.' She said nothing about her experiences in the garden the previous night: whatever it was she thought she had heard or seen could only have been in her imagination.

'It *is* a bit different from home here, I know,' said her mother. 'The house and garden have loads of atmosphere, haven't they? And we're not really Tessa and Tony Swift's sort of people, are we? I wasn't very happy with that crowd last night myself, but I think some of them have already gone. They'd just come to dinner. I heard at least two cars drive off after we'd gone upstairs. There should be a more family group left now: easier to fit into. I'm hoping that sometime this afternoon or tomorrow morning I can settle down to making some sketches. I know Tessa would love me to do that. It's going to be a perfect day when the sun gets up properly. Just look at that white frost! I should be able to take lots of colour photographs with any luck.'

'That's funny,' exclaimed Josephine who had not been listening to her mother very closely. 'Daddy, did you say Mrs Swift was driving the Spanish people to Mass? I think I heard her go downstairs about an hour ago. It must have been long after that when I saw their little girl again looking through the door at me. I went to the bathroom and must have left it open and I saw her standing in the doorway as if she wanted to come in. I said "hullo" but then she went away. First of all I thought she was some relation of the Swifts, but she wasn't with them at all later on, so when I saw her again I thought she might be the Spanish couple's child. She's dark, you see. Pale and dark. I'd have thought they'd have taken her with them. She wasn't that young. About seven or eight, I should think.'

'I haven't heard that the Spanish couple have a child,' said her mother. 'But they could, I suppose. They might have left her behind: after all there are plenty of people in the house to look after her.'

'I suppose so,' said Josephine doubtfully. Something didn't quite fit: next time she saw the little girl she determined to speak to her. Then she heard a noise of feet and laughter upon the stairs: some of the boys were coming down, and she forgot all about the little girl who seemed rather attracted to her, or to her room.

What a strange Christmas Day it was. Breakfast was a help-yourself meal with people wandering in and out of the dining room, and afterwards Josephine and her mother helped Greta and Tessa Swift to clear the plates away. While she was doing this she found that the four-year old Annabella had taken a fancy to her.

'Come and play with me, Josephine,' she nagged. 'Come and see my room.'

'Oh, all right.' Josephine gave in to her at last. As she carried the last tray of crockery into the kitchen she looked about for the little girl who must belong to the Spanish couple. But there was no sign of her or of them.

'Where are the Spanish people?' she asked Annabella casually.

'Don't know. In their flat I expect.' Annabella pointed down the passage to a door.

'Come *on*, Josephine.'

'Oh, all right,' and Josephine went.

Then it was time to walk to church and in the end quite a large party of people, headed by Tony Swift, flourishing a walking stick, made their way up the oak avenue and thence onto a public footpath between a double hedge and along a lane to the village. The frost lay like a thick white icing over everything: there was enough of it to scrape off the leaves and to taste.

The church service made Josephine feel incredibly hungry. She wanted to eat more than the frost on the way back. She and Jason, who evidently felt much the same, walked rapidly ahead of the rest of the party.

'Present-giving next,' said Jason, breaking into a trot up the steps. 'Let's hope it doesn't take too long.'

They were all organized by Tessa Swift into the sitting room where a great many parcels of all shapes and sizes were piled about the tree.

'Come on, come on,' she cried. 'Everybody gives everybody else their presents all together. And then we all have lunch in the dining room. I've laid two tables in there. Josephine, I'm going to start with you. Catch!'

'Oh! Thank you very much, it's awfully kind of you,' said Josephine, embarrassed and rather overwhelmed, undoing the wrapping paper to disclose a large electric torch.

'Now mine to Annabella ...' and so the present-giving went on and on. Josephine was amazed at the amount the other children got. Little Annabella had a Walkie Talkie doll and an enormous teddy bear bigger than herself, and both she and her sister had dressing-up costumes and wigs with false hair, besides innumerable games and books. The boys had yet more elaborate games: footballs, things that wound up and down, whirred and howled, chemistry sets —and soon the floor was knee deep in wrapping paper and string, and boxes of chocolates and candies littered every seat and surface. It was too much, and Josephine would have preferred to be quietly at home and not have everyone see her present to her father, a pen: to her mother, eight different reels of cotton in a little round drum, and theirs to her: a book she had long wanted and a shoulder bag with a purse inside and a pound note with the purse. She wondered if Tessa and Tony Swift knew her father was redundant and they could not afford much this Christmas? And then she felt ashamed of herself for being a little embarrassed and ashamed and tried hard to forget her horrible self-consciousness for a time and to be full of Christmas spirit towards everyone and everybody.

Christmas spirit would work a good deal better for a good Christmas dinner inside one: it was all very well for the grown-ups: they had been swigging sherry for the past hour.

Tony Swift, bright pink in the face, was already immensely jolly and paused in his task of carving the turkey to seize the pretty Janey's bare arm and kiss it from wrist to shoulder, smacking his lips and saying heartily,

'Yum, yum, I should like to eat it all up.'

'Really,' thought Josephine rather primly, disapproving, 'if he's got to eat someone he should be eating his own wife.'

But Tessa didn't seem to mind: with one hand she wielded spoonfuls of sprouts, with another, little sausages, and in between this she found time to dig her husband in the ribs with the handle of the spoon and say,

'Oh get on carving Tony do, for heaven's sake.'

At last the long meal was over.

'All right, don't say it, Aunt Tessa. I know what we've got to do.' Rob got up and stretched.

'Not clear the table!' cried his younger brother in horror. 'Oh no! I'm too full! I'd drop everything.'

'Yes we're going to, you just leave it to us, Aunt Tessa.'

Rob had a kind of genial authority at times. He was a strong character, the kind of boy who is chosen as a prefect, and soon had his team organized while the adult members of the party left the room with what Josephine thought to be a rather unnecessary haste.

She and Jason began to stack plates, while Simon with a rather cross look about him took a tray to load up with glasses. Josephine was glad that Miranda was helping him and not herself; she was still cautious of Simon and yet she could not altogether forget him and ignore him. Indeed it was not long before he began to stir things up in what she was beginning to realize was his usual manner.

'Oh I'm tired of this clearing away,' he suddenly said, dumping his third tray of glasses in the kitchen. 'Why should *we* tidy up after all *their* drinks? They shouldn't have had so much sherry and wine and stuff. I'm always finding an extra glass somewhere and it's a *bore*. I'm packing it in. Rupert, give us a go with that vampire bat thing, will you? Tell you what, would you like to do a swop with me? I don't like that motor boat I got. I've another at home. I'll swop you that for the bat.'

'The little bat or the big one?' asked Rupert, narrowing his eyes in a sharp look. He had been given two: wound up they flapped their wings and gnashed their grossly out-of-proportion fangs and had a kind of fascination for everybody.

'Don't do it, Rupert,' warned his older brother. 'Swops hardly ever work out. Daddy forbade them last year.'

'I don't mind if it's the little one.' Rupert was obviously tempted.

'Tell you what, I'll—'

Josephine didn't hear the rest of the conversation but details of the swop, soon grown more and more elaborate, obtruded themselves for the rest of the day.

Of course it did go wrong, for the motor-boat was found to be broken. Simon said Rupert had broken it himself by careless treatment. Rupert and Rob retorted together that it must have been broken by Simon and that was why he had wanted to part with it. The quarrel muttered and mounted: finally breaking out with thundering fury across the hall just as Tony Swift was coming into it from the sitting room.

'Blooming beastly noisy little ruffians!' he suddenly erupted. 'Give us a break, can't you? Come on, upstairs the whole pack of you!'

'Me too?' enquired Josephine, who had been standing, an interested looker-on, at the foot of the stairs.

'Yes! All of you! Upstairs this instant!'

'Hateful man,' thought Josephine, her dignity much wounded. That he should lump her, who had been doing nothing wrong and intended to do nothing wrong, with those quarrelling boys seemed to her especially unfair. She had not liked him and she had been right. He was rude and coarse and lacked discrimination. She would have brooded longer over this, but little Annabella seized her and bore her off to her playroom to inspect her dolls. Once there Josephine made good the opportunity to ride Miranda and Annabella's rocking-horse. It was a beautiful big one and though she knew she was rather elderly for such pleasures she had been casting covetous eyes on it ever since she had first seen it.

'You can make it move forward if you make it rock hard enough.' Jason put his head in through the open door. 'Come on, I'll show you.' He progressed about the room in jerks, rocking frenziedly to and fro.

'There's a hunt tomorrow,' he informed Josephine suddenly. 'They're meeting in the village. Rob and Rupert and I have a plan on. I told you we were going to *do* something about Simon, didn't I? Well, we're going to hunt him, and when we catch him we'll string him up. That motor-boat's broken completely now and he's also spoilt Rupe's bat.'

'But suppose he doesn't want to be hunted and won't run?' asked Josephine.

'Oh, he wants to be hunted all right. The point is, he thinks it's just good fun. But we're *serious*. He'll suffer when we catch him. Want to join in?'

'I don't know,' replied Josephine dubiously. 'I'd rather watch the other hunt, the proper hunt.'

'Huh! Gees-gees—dogs—lots of silly people all dolled up and thinking themselves the cat's whiskers. You can *keep* that sort of hunt as far as I'm concerned,' Jason told her scornfully.

'By the way, Jason, there was something I wanted to ask you, or somebody. Have *you* seen a dark little girl about upstairs, she's perhaps a little younger than Miranda? Is she the daughter of the Spanish couple?'

'Dark girl,' he said, between jerks. 'Ouf. I think I'll ride this horse to death if I go on. No. I haven't seen any other girl, apart from you and Miranda and Annabella. Isn't that enough?'

'Funny,' said Josephine uneasily. 'But I suppose the Spanish people could have a little girl, without your having noticed her?'

'I suppose so,' he said, not very interested. '*I* don't know. They're different from the couple Tessa had last year. They were Portuguese. Why don't you ask Miranda, or Tessa herself?'

'Of course I could do that,' said Josephine, feeling a little foolish. 'Only it was easier, somehow, to ask you.'

'Well, I'm off,' announced Jason, dismounting, and leaving Josephine uncertain as to whether he wanted her to follow him or not. She still felt she did not know the boys well enough to intrude upon their games. So she spent an increasingly boring hour in the playroom until her mother came to fetch her with the words, 'Come along, Josephine,

33

Tessa wants us all to gather together and sing carols round the Christmas tree.'

Josephine must have been overtired by the late night and a long, rather unsatisfactory day or she would not have replied as disagreeably as she did:

'Oh, no! I *hate* carols, we got enough of them at the end of term.'

'Oh, come on Josephine,' said her mother, shepherding her into her room to untie her plaits and do them up again more neatly. 'Do try and look as though you're enjoying yourself even if you aren't! You've got a face like a sour prune.'

'*I* didn't ask Tessa Swift to ask me here to this horrid uncomfortable house and spoil my Christmas for me,' muttered Josephine in the kind of voice which is meant to be overheard.

'I think you are most spoilt and ungrateful,' said her mother acidly.

Silence: they emerged onto the landing glaring at one another in true mother and daughter fashion and then were forced to descend the stairs looking as good-tempered as possible, for Tessa Swift was standing in the hall.

'Here we are!' called Mrs Palmer in the brightest and cheeriest of tones.

'Here I am at Cold Christmas on Christmas Day,' wrote Josephine in her diary that night. 'We went to church in the morning and then had presents round the tree.' She described her presents.

'For Christmas dinner we had turkey as you might expect.' She paused: should she add anything more? 'A rather heavy day' she put at last. Not a very inspired entry, but still ...

'And now I shall read my book,' she thought, thankfully putting down her pen.

Three pages were turned, then Josephine's head sank low upon her pillow and her eyes closed despite themselves. She came back to full consciousness with a jerk and began to get out of bed to turn out the light by the door, as there was no bedside lamp. And again, as she had described to her parents that morning, she saw the little dark girl in her room. This time she must have crept in as Josephine nodded, for she was standing with her back to the drawn curtains at the window, looking at Josephine and smiling shyly.

'Hullo!' said Josephine, a little startled. 'I never saw you come in. Do you want anything? What is your name?'

The child did not reply. For the first time Josephine had time to look at her properly. She was wearing a long white cotton nightdress nearly down to her ankles. It had a high neck with some rather grubby lace about the collar. The nightdress itself looked as if it could have done with a wash as could the little girl's long tangled dark hair. Her nose was running slightly and looked a little red. Nevertheless she had an appealing face, if on the thin and peaky side Her feet were grimy and bare. She put out a hand towards Josephine's best wool dress which was lying over the chair and Josephine got the very strong impression that she wanted to say something, but was too shy.

'Do you like it?' asked Josephine eventually. 'Would you like to try it on?'

The child looked at her and smiled, and nodded, again looking as if she very much wanted to speak. Josephine's eyes flicked back to her book for a moment and when she looked again the little girl was gone.

'That was quick,' she said out loud to herself to dispel a slight feeling of unease. 'I must have scared her away. I expect she doesn't understand English.'

She wished she knew what the silly little thing wanted, and how she had entered and left her room so silently, and then she got out of bed and turned out the light.

Many hours later, just before dawn, Josephine opened her eyes and found herself struggling to remember all the details of one of the most disturbing and emotional dreams she had ever experienced. The strange thing was that she had not been herself, Josephine Palmer. She was perfectly clear about that. She had been called Margaret; she had slept in the room in which she now was, there was a wardrobe in much the same place but the bed was different. It had four wooden posts and a canopy overhead which sagged in the middle. The bed itself was stuffy and hard and she had tossed and turned and ached. Then she had got up because she had already tried calling and calling until her throat was sore, and nobody had come. The candle by her bed had sunk to a little splutter and it was very dark but she had taken it in her hand and gone a long, long way, groping in the dark down the stairs, across the freezing hall, towards the passage and the kitchen beyond. In the kitchen she would find Betty and Betty might help. Betty might give her a soothing drink and sit by her bed awhile. It was no use going for anyone else because her mother and father were at their London house and had taken some of the servants with them. The Josephine who was also this little girl called Margaret was just sufficiently also Josephine at this point to realize that the house smelt and felt quite different: there was more heavy furniture in it: more statuary and curtains although she could hardly see them. Large shapes loomed and creaked in the flickering light. And somehow although she was near no window and it was dark anyway she knew that trees, tangled miles of them, approached near to the house on its west side.

At last she was in the kitchen which shone with a red glow from the fire in a kitchen range all along one wall. And Josephine/Margaret realized with a shock and yet also a kind of remembrance that it wasn't going to be any good. Betty wouldn't, couldn't help her because Betty her nurse was drunk, and so was Alice the cook. It had happened before, not once, but several times. Betty who was buxom and blonde sat giggling stupidly on one side of the fire, her face red and her cap half off, showing her yellow locks straggling down over her collar. Alice, who was a rough, hard woman of whom Margaret was frightened, sat snoring opposite her, her head lolling stupidly.

'Wha—do yer—want 'ere?' Betty was just capable of saying, laughing stupidly as she did so. 'Ge—back a bed—afore I—tan yer backside.'

'Don't be like that, Betty,' Margaret/Josephine found herself pleading. 'Please Betty, come upstairs with me. Please Betty, be my nice Betty.'

There was a long moment of anguish: of knowledge that she was ill and abandoned: of longing for a mother she had difficulty in remembering clearly, and then Josephine became Josephine and woke.

'Oh, oh,' she shuddered to herself. And then she thought: 'But of course that would never happen to *me*. Thank heavens it was only a dream!'

Only a dream, but yet something more. It was the feelings that lasted longest: the suffocating loneliness; the stuffiness, chill and oppression of the dark house, the desperate wish for comfort which she half knew would not come. The child in Josephine's dream had been ill: really ill, not just miserable, and this gave the dream an added dimension of seriousness and horror.

She sat up in bed and thought about it. It was just beginning to get light, and she could see enough from her window to realize that outside there was a white, freezing mist. She pulled her eiderdown about her and looked out. The trees had disappeared: the garden had disappeared, she could not even see the ground below nor the windows of her parents' bedroom some feet further along. She could see a little of the wall surrounding her own window—then nothing. There was a muffled, dead feeling to the air: nothing stirred.

'I am all alone,' thought Josephine. 'If I were to shout and scream no one would hear me. I am like a princess in an enchanted tower.'

She knew perfectly well she had only to open her bedroom door and everything would appear normal, but this she did not want to do. Normality, people, light, noise could muffle the clear voices of what lay underneath. There *were* underneath things in this house, and outside it. The house, so white, so resonant with sound, had not always been so. The country outside, neat and orderly compared to what it once had been nevertheless retained ... a something. It had not altogether been imagination on the night of Christmas Eve, and her dream—had her dream been altogether a dream?

It was as if the little girl Margaret had existed and she had met her. It was as if she herself had been Margaret in another life. It was as if—

'I wish I could have helped her,' she thought confusedly. 'I wish I could have been upstairs with her, and talked to her and told her stories. I could have made her laugh; I could have made her feel less lonely. And yet how could I, if in some way I *was* her?

'I must have another try at talking to the little Spanish girl,' she thought next. 'I must ask Miranda about her, not

Annabella who is too young to bother to answer questions when she's not interested. I *could* ask Mrs Swift. Except that—I don't want to. But someone will know her. Of course they will.'

It was only two thirds of Josephine who thought thus and thus. The last part of her kept still, looking through the closed window out into the mist and knowing the answer perfectly well.

# 4

Day again: proper bright day, the sun breaking through: it would be many-coloured and brilliant and there was no time for anything but here and now.

'Are you coming with us to see the hunt meet?' said Josephine's parents to her. 'It's only a mile away, Tessa says, on the village green. It's a grand day for it.'

The village green was packed with people, cars and horses: the horses, giant, sleek, gleaming beasts wove and pirouetted between the cars, which were either stationary or proceeding at a snail's pace.

'Look, there's Miranda on her pony!' exclaimed Josephine, riven with deep envy. Some people had all the luck: here was the spoiled Miranda, a child at least three years younger than herself, showing complete mastery over her pony and about to enjoy the excitement of the hunt. Even though Josephine didn't exactly approve of hunts and hoped the fox would escape she nevertheless longed to ride. Yet she could not ask for riding lessons now—when they had to count every penny.

'Tessa looks splendid, doesn't she?' commented Mrs Palmer.

'She seems to sit her horse so naturally, as if it were part of her,' agreed her husband. 'She's certainly in her element here.'

Josephine then noticed Tony Swift, who sat his big bay gelding firmly enough, and yet who did not seem so much at home as his wife. He called out a few remarks to other people on horseback, but it was Tessa, severe and remote-looking in her bowler, whom everybody seemed to know best.

Josephine wondered why people on horseback had such haughty expressions. She both disliked and envied them : an odd, unsettling emotion.

Little scraps of conversation floated down. 'He's going like a bomb this season and so—'

'A little weakness in the hock.'

'We had an absolutely fantastic run last week.'

'Hope there isn't too much wire that way.'

'She's an absolutely super little mare, isn't she?'

'It should be reasonably soft going now the sun's up. Lucky the frost isn't deep in.'

They began to move off and through the thinning crowd Josephine caught sight of Rob and Jason, deep in conversation. They looked important, excited.

Of course the boys have their own hunt, she thought, not very interested.

They were going : hounds and horses were streaming off down the road.

'Ah well,' said Mr Palmer, beating his hands together. 'Let's walk to the top of the hill and see if we can see them across the fields.'

'I wonder what time lunch is,' said Josephine. 'When will Mrs Swift get back?'

'Oh, we're to have a help-yourself cold lunch, I believe, at any time between one and two. Then they've got more people coming in for drinks and a hot meal this evening.'

41

'*More* people,' cried Josephine, horrified. 'I suppose I have to have my supper with those boys again. Thank goodness we go home tomorrow.'

'Well, darling, Tessa actually pressed us to stay another day, so we go back the day after *that*. I need a little more time for my painting and apparently they've a big treasure hunt for you children planned tomorrow. Tessa said you can't possibly miss that.'

'Oh, can't I? Suppose I don't *want* their silly treasure hunt,' muttered Josephine rebelliously. 'I'd much rather go home tomorrow. Wouldn't you? I thought you were so cold in bed here.'

'Tessa banged away at our radiator and at last it came on. Shall I ask her to do the same for yours? I'm sorry, darling. It was *so* difficult not to accept, it really was.'

'People shouldn't go about asking people to stay with them against their will,' grumbled Josephine.

'You're not *really* disliking it here, are you?' asked her father with one of his penetrating looks.

'Well, no, not exactly. The evenings, the nights, well, they're—' Josephine's voice died away. 'It's just that during the day it's so sort of *bitty*: I don't know what's going to happen next. And I'm sort of half with the boys and half not. And Miranda is really too young for me.'

'I understand that. Still I think you can bear one more day, when it's helpful to your mother's plans, can't you?'

'Yes, Daddy.' There was nothing else to say when he spoke to her like that: she might as well shut up.

'Look, there they go!'

Hounds, horses, a few hangers-on running behind them, were spreading out at a canter over the frozen fields, the ploughed land scattered with the remains of frost like chocolate cake with a white icing, down into a valley, along beside a ditch and then into a wood. The thin yet stirring sound of a horn came from the wood. Soon they were all out of sight.

Josephine, feeling she was missing out on a lot of excitement as she so often did, continued the sedate walk with her parents which brought them in a half circle to return down the oak avenue to the house. Somewhere behind a tree she saw a flicker of something grey: a boy.

'You go on in,' she told her parents. 'I'm going to muck about out here for a while.'

A good deal of time went by: the sun was fully up now, the sky a beautiful pale blue and it was almost warm amongst the trunks of trees and dead leaves which caught the full sun. It was a pity the lake was not frozen deep enough yet for safe sliding. The glimpse of boy did not resolve itself into anything further until much later, when at the far end of the avenue Josephine saw Rob, Rupert and Jason running together.

'Have you seen him?' they shouted as soon as they were in earshot.

'No, I don't think so. I wondered if I didn't see one of you over there somewhere about half an hour ago but I looked around and there was nobody.'

'Oh, blast!' Rob was obviously out of humour. 'Come on you men, let's beat around the lake.'

'We must get him, we must get him,' cried Rupert shrilly.

'Oh, shut your gob, Rupe. You get on my nerves yelling like that. Come on, Jason.'

'What are you going to do to him when you get him?' asked Josephine curiously.

'Never you mind.' Jason pushed past her. 'This way, Rob. You go this way and I'll go the other.'

Really: something seemed to have got into them, all

three: a tense, rather bad tempered excitement; she wanted no part of it.

'I'm going to have some lunch,' announced Josephine in a loud voice. 'It's after one.' But they had gone, crackling into the undergrowth at the lake's side.

So she left them to their own devices.

In the house she found several people in the dining room walking about and eating. Tony and Miranda had returned but there was no sign of Tessa. Josephine was a little surprised that it was he and not his wife who had brought Miranda home, but apparently Tessa was always in at the death, if there was a death.

'It was lovely,' Miranda kept saying, her eyes shining. 'Snowball galloped and galloped and we jumped a hedge. Daddy nearly fell off.'

'Nonsense, brat,' said her father. 'I was merely re-arranging myself in the saddle a little. I have to keep up with my riding. I'm having a long sequence on horseback this New Year sometime, aren't I, Bill?' This was to Jason's father who laughed and said he was sure Tony would do him credit.

'I can't say the same for one or two of the others,' he said to Josephine's father. 'These period dramas can be the very devil to get the horse riding bits right. We had one bloke who *kept* falling off in one series I produced. I got him quiet horses, I did everything bar glue him to his seat, but we lost so much time, re-shooting, I vowed never to use him again.'

At last Rob, Rupert and Jason appeared, hot, tired and dirty, to tear ravenously at the cold turkey, but there was no sign of Simon and no one had seen him. The hunters had entirely lost their quarry.

After lunch the boys vanished, obviously to search about for Simon. Josephine went out into the garden and saw no trace of them. She felt restless again, out of things. Acting on a sudden idea, she walked down towards the beginning of the oak trees. The avenue was deserted. But she *had* seen something grey earlier and Simon was wearing grey trousers. As silently as she could she walked between the trees, pausing every now and then. Then she heard a sound, distinctly. She took another pace or two and listened. An eating sound. The tree on her left was eating.

This was plainly ridiculous; but it was a hollow tree. Through a hole near the roots she saw something moving. The eating sound continued.

That was Simon's lair. He must have seized some food early on, and retired to it. However long did he mean to stay there?

Josephine did not surprise him but swung on her heel and returned. She was nearly back to the house when she found Rob, Rupert and Jason wandering about on the upper lawn.

'Want to know where he is?' she said, teasing them. Her instincts would have been with the hunted, except that he had been unpleasant to her and obviously deserved whatever was coming. So she let them draw Simon's whereabouts out of her little by little.

'Right,' said Rob, the self-imposed captain, at the end of it. '*Now* we'll get him.'

Intent upon their prey they ran off while Josephine went inside, already repenting of what she had done. Something told her she should have let them work it out for themselves.

It was much later. Josephine, Miranda, Annabella together with the Swedish au pair Greta, had a polite tea in the sitting room with various other members of the party. Going across the hall later on Josephine caught a glimpse of Rob and Rupert climbing the stairs. Oh good, she thought with relief. The boys had obviously finished their game, or whatever it was, and come in.

She went into her room without putting on the light although it was now dusk. She had a half hope of finding— somebody there. If she walked gently she would not frighten her away. But the room was empty, the curtains undrawn and the just risen moon shining in. Again it was very cold. The sun had gone but there was still a red light streaking through a band of dark cloud above where it had set. The rest of the sky was steely blue and the stars were out.

The garden and the trees beyond and the fields beyond that were intensely beautiful in this cold half-light. The sky was a sky of drama, of meaning, a sky which demanded one's attention. It was so different here, at Cold Christmas, from home in a suburban road on the outskirts of an over- grown village with houses all about. Here there was space and quiet.

Josephine opened the window wide and looked out. And there, with a shock, she saw him. Down the stone steps and by the frozen pond. A tied figure, standing absolutely still, arms outstretched in the attitude of a scarecrow. His head lolled upon his shoulders: this she could see plainly. He was too still, and it was too cold and a dreadful thrill of fear transfixed Josephine. Simon had been tied too long and had frozen to death and it was partly her fault! Were Jason and Rob and Rupert and she *killers*? It was a kind of nightmare she was in: it couldn't be happening.

She ran out of the room and into Jason who was just passing.

'Oh look, Jason, come quick, what have you done?' she cried, dragging him to the window. 'Simon has frozen!'

'He couldn't have.' Jason looked out of the window and stiffened. 'He can't still be there. He *can't*.'

'You did then! You *did* tie him up like that!'

'Yes, we tied him all right but with easy granny knots. Anybody could have worked their way out in five minutes and Simon is clever! But we did it *ages* ago. The sun was still out. Hasn't he come back yet?'

'No, he's *there*, Jason. You can see him. Where is Rob? What is he doing?'

'Oh, Rob is up with Rupert in his bedroom, reading to him. Rupert had earache and Tessa sent him to bed with a hot water bottle. Rupert gets earache if he gets very cold.'

'And what about *Simon*?' cried Josephine. 'What does *he* get? Oh God, Jason, what have you done?'

'It's impossible,' said Jason, visibly shaken. 'Come on. We'd better get out to him. Josephine—don't tell anybody else, *please*, but just come with me and see.'

'All right—'

Josephine snatched up the torch which Tessa had given her for a Christmas present and they ran outside.

'It can't be, it can't be,' Jason was muttering as he ran, 'it just *can't*. It was hours ago. Somebody would have seen him if he'd been there all that time.'

'Jason—*something must have happened*,' cried Josephine with a face of horror. 'I know—something is *happening*.'

'I don't know what you mean—'

'I don't myself except that—oh, Jason—'

She grabbed at him and they stood stock still, looking at Simon.

'It's nothing like,' cried Jason in relief. 'Quick, shine the torch.'

A crumpled nothing face of paper under an anorak hood. empty trousers, empty sleeves, with wooden ends sticking out of them—yet it had given them a terrible shock. Jason pulled up the cross-piece of wood and shook it and it disintegrated into ends of broomsticks and sundry garments.

47

'He must have done it himself to give us a fright. He's probably hiding somewhere near and laughing at us,' he said.

'How perfectly nasty.' Josephine shuddered. Eyes, malign eyes, were all about them. And yet—it had been three—or four—if you counted her part in it—against one. It had not been fair. And he had but taken a good revenge.

'How did you tie him?'

'Well, we *meant* to tie him something like that,' Jason admitted. 'You see we found this old scarecrow in the stables and that gave us the idea. We took the body off of course—it was just a sack and a cap—and meant to use the cross-stick. But the ground was so frozen he'd have jerked the stick out in a moment, we couldn't get it in any way at all. So though we had the stick all ready, in the end tied him to that little tree, there. That's what had me a bit puzzled. You could see him—it—from your window but not the tree. In fact the hedge partly hides it. And he must have gone in for other clothes. Those are the trousers he *was* wearing.'

'A clever trick,' said Josephine, shivering. 'He took us in, all right.'

'He took *you* in all right.'

'Oh, Jason, you know you were tricked too. And now where is he? Shall we call to him?'

'All right. Simon!'

'Simon!' Josephine echoed him. They both of them wanted now to establish contact: not to have this eerie stillness about them: this possibly hostile watcher.

'Whi-whoo,' a heavy body flew past them, startling them. Otherwise there was silence.

'There's something scuttering about down there,' said Jason suddenly. 'In the bushes.'

'Simon! Come on out! The laugh's on you!'

The something in the bushes ran towards them, with eyes glittering like jewels in the torchlight, and wagging its rear end. It was Susie, the poodle, delighted to see them.

*Now* I shall be taken for a proper walk seemed to be her attitude as she capered about them.

She gave them both courage and a feeling of normality.

'Let's just go down to the oak avenue and the lake,' said Jason. 'And if we don't find him there we'll leave him to stew in his own juice. Perhaps he's back in the house by now, anyway.'

'Perhaps, but I don't feel so,' said Josephine. She was rather apprehensive that Simon was going to jump out at her in some horrid way, but nevertheless she followed Jason. He was a reassuring person to have about.

'Jason, why is Simon so unpleasant?' she found it possible to ask.

'Oh well,' he replied tolerantly, 'I suppose he's not as bad as all that really. It's just that he won't join in often and he's bad at losing and he likes teasing people. I expect it's not his fault. He's an only child and his mother—she's Tessa's older sister—his mother spoils him terribly. If there's anything that's just the very latest thing Simon always has to have it. He's a bit that kind of person.'

'*I* know,' said Josephine. Yet this summary did not contain the essence of Simon, she thought to herself. Someone like Simon could always elude the understanding of someone like Jason or Rob: she knew this too. They had not handled Simon well—and now, what more would happen?

'Oh, what's that?' She clutched suddenly at Jason. For the most eerie, melancholy cry she had ever heard in her life was echoing harshly through the night.

'Ee—har! ee—har!'

Then it stopped as suddenly as it had begun.

49

'Never heard a donkey hee-haw before?' asked Jason, in kindly scorn.

'Yes of course. At least, I don't know. Not like that ...' she said weakly, feeling a fool. She had forgotten, or never knew. She had thought that donkeys were part of the cosy, nursery world of baa-ing sheep and clucking hens: not creatures to tear the night apart with cries as of a lost soul.

She was now shivering all over, though she was not, apart from her gloveless hands, particularly cold. It was a kind of nervous excitement: she felt it sometimes before parties or before thunder, but this was worse.

'Listen, do you hear anything?' she said suddenly, clutching Jason's arm.

'No. What should I hear now, for heaven's sake?'

'It sounded like horses' hooves: pounding some way away.'

'Can't hear a thing. Mind that branch, you idiot.'

'Hell's teeth,' said Josephine, entangled in it. It had become a good deal darker, and now they were under the trees. There were some very black shadows. The lake nearby glistened in starlight. A dark shape detached itself from the side of a tumbledown boathouse she had not particularly noticed before.

'Who is it?' came a quavering voice.

'Simon? It's us—what are you doing?' called Jason in evident relief.

Simon half ran, half walked towards them.

Why, he's *scared*, thought Josephine. He's scared to death.

Simon came up to stand near them. He even bent and fondled Susie, and seemed to find a comfort from their presence.

'Did you see anything?' he asked.

'No, what?' asked Josephine, casually swinging her torch

round in great arcs. 'What should we have seen?'

'I don't know. At least—there was something. Something running. From the house and up the avenue. It—well, it was scaring. And when I saw you, I thought, well, I thought, here's some more of them.'

'More of *what*?' demanded Jason, obviously at sea. 'And what on earth are you holding?'

Simon looked at what dangled from his hand as if he had forgotten all about it. 'Oh, this dead hare,' he said in a puzzled way, as if he were seeing it for the first time. 'I was messing about and I found it near a tree trunk. It seemed such a shame somehow to leave it there, but I don't know what to do with it. It's quite stiff, look.'

'Poor thing,' said Josephine sympathetically. Susie beside her suddenly reared up and touched it with her nose.

'*I* don't want it,' said Simon suddenly. He brought his arm back and launched the hare in a great curved throw over the surface of the lake. It hit with a plunk and skidded crazily this way and that over the ice until it was lost in darkness.

'You needn't have done that,' said Josephine uneasily.

'I don't get it,' said Jason suddenly, as they turned to leave the lake side. 'What scared you and what were you doing down here? We found the scarecrow and it was quite good, I'll give you that. Were you expecting us to follow you?'

'Well, yes, sort of.'

Simon was still a little shaky, but gradually they got his story out of him. He had intended to stay near his scarecrow and jump out and frighten whoever came to investigate it. But his plans went wrong because it was a long time being discovered and he grew cold and bored. And so he had wandered down to the oak avenue and the lake. And then he had begun to imagine things—as a joke at first. He had wondered what would happen if the scarecrow he had made came waddling after him.

'You've been reading *The Enchanted Castle*: the Ugly Wugs,' said Josephine at this point.

'No I haven't, I've never heard of it. But, well, I just wished I hadn't thought of scarecrows at all, the old rags moving and that kind of thing. And I'll absolutely swear I heard something moving around the lake, on the other side of the boathouse, where the trees and bushes come right down to the water. And then there was a creepy sort of cry: but I suppose it could have been an owl.'

'*We* heard an owl,' said Jason. 'I expect there was another one answering it.'

'*I* don't know,' said Simon, his voice still shaky. 'And then, after the owl, or whatever it was, there came a sort of panting and a noise of hooves, coming from the other direction, from the house. And I didn't like it, it was beastly.'

'*I* heard hooves,' cried Josephine. 'Do you remember, Jason?'

Simon looked at her and it was as if a very faint salutation passed between them.

'Then I saw something moving up near the house, I don't know what it was. And the trees. The trees were different. It was only a moment.'

'The *trees* were different? How do you mean?' asked Jason.

'I don't know.' Simon shook his head in bewilderment. 'There suddenly seemed to be more of them.'

'Oh, come on, let's get back before you imagine anything else,' said Jason impatiently.

'Tell me more about the trees,' said Josephine almost at the same moment.

'Oh, it's no use. You can't understand how odd it was

suddenly.' Simon was beginning to recover himself. 'I'd been alone too long: you were such a beastly long time finding my scarecrow.'

They were between the last few oaks now: nearly at the beginning of the bottom part of the garden, where it had been let go and the long frosted grass and weeds tangled together.

'Wait,' said Josephine. 'My shoelace is undone.' She bent to it and then she saw Susie. Susie the poodle bitch was crouching to the ground, and she was quivering all over.

'What's the matter with Susie?' cried Josephine urgently, and it was then that Simon clutched her.

'It's beginning again,' he said in a quiet, dried-up voice.

# 5

There were hoofbeats, the soft squelchy noise of some heavy horse cantering over grass, and the creak of harness.

'Oh but it's just somebody—one of Tessa's horses, one of the hunt,' began Josephine weakly, but was stopped by Simon's hiss. 'It *isn't*, don't be stupid. And look back to the house. Look at the trees. It's just as it was when I was alone, only it's stronger. Oh God, what is happening?'

Josephine looked up the terraced hill of the garden, towards the house. The house was dark. She could only just see the shape of it. There was one light but it must be a light held in somebody's hand, bobbing about near the front door. And every now and then this light went out—was extinguished from view, because of the trees. The person who was holding it was moving and the trees ... There should not be trees. But there were. The avenue led right up to the house now. The terraced garden was gone. The avenue led in a curve, to avoid the steepest part of the hill, nearly to the door pillars. The trees were taller too. They were different kinds: some oak, some elm. Some of the trees were young, half-grown only. She had not time to get more than a fleeting impression of the difference of it all because then a horse galloped round the curve of the avenue into their view. It was a rough clod-hopping animal, not a proper riding horse. It was obvious that it was not used to being ridden; that it probably usually pulled a cart.

On its back, riding badly, right up on its withers, was a shabby-looking youth. The horse plunged its head, tried to buck, and he whopped it with a stick and it bounded on, rolling its eyes, with its ears back. It passed close by where they stood, huddled together, but the youth did not turn his head or give any sign that he had seen them. He had just passed them by a few feet down the centre of the avenue when it seemed as though a tree split in half; a tall tree, with no warning beyond a slow, splintering, cracking noise, shed an enormous branch which fell before the rider. He was not quite in time to avoid it: the horse reared, the lad was half thrown, half knocked from the saddle by one of the lesser branches falling with the greater one. The avenue was now blocked by a dark mass of wood. The horse ran off, kicking and jumping in fright, the saddle twisted under its belly. The youth lay in a huddled heap upon the ground. He stirred but did not get up.

There was no time to move or speak or think: the vision continued. Something now approached from the other direction, driving up the avenue towards the house. A horse-drawn vehicle: lit by lamps, one on each side. It came to a sudden halt, blocked by the fallen wood, and Josephine could see it was a carriage of some kind, with a pair of horses, people within, and a man in livery before and behind.

Susie was still quivering all over and whining: she crept to Josephine as if for comfort but Josephine could give her none. These people were not real, were not people of here and now. What had happened here once? What was being reenacted before their eyes? What had set it all off?

One of the strangest things of all was that no voice could be heard, though there had been sounds enough: sounds made by the horse, by the tree falling, by the carriage and pair. There should—would have been—human shouts, but they did not get through.

In silence the coachman jumped from his seat and ran to the horses' heads; in silence the other servant wrenched at the branches and pointed to the youth lying beyond. One of the men then ran round behind the trees and approached the fallen youth who struggled to a sitting position. But all was quiet, except the swaying and knocking of branches as if there were a high wind. The light from the carriage lamps shone patchily through the fallen branches, making confusing pools of light and shade. Yet one could see that words of some kind must have been shouted back to the people within the carriage because suddenly a woman leapt from it, her bonnet half off, and without seeming to realize that by going between the tree trunks she could skirt the fallen branches, she pushed right through, squeezing half up against the tree that had split, twigs from the fallen branches scraping at her dress and cloak. With a pull and a wrench she was through and running past the children with a distraught expression upon her face. It was a pretty, rather silly face, not unlike Tony Swift's friend Janey, Josephine noticed. A man appeared now: a gentleman in boots and a long cloak: his mouth moved as he called after her, but no sound came. He staggered a little and shrugged his shoulders and waited for two more people to catch him up; another finely dressed lady and gentleman. They took little notice of the unfortunate youth, now struggling to rise, but slowly and unsteadily as though they were all a little tipsy began to walk up the drive. They stumbled by the children, talking hard and laughing in a rather vacant, drunken way from time to time, but no voices could be heard. The sound of wind increased until all the branches were swaying and roaring together and now no other sound

56

at all penetrated: when the horses were finally unharnessed and led round behind the trees because there was no room for the carriage to pass, there came no sound of hooves: *ghosts*, they paced up between the trees, led by the two menservants. The injured youth had been lifted and sat the second horse; in silence they passed the horror-struck children; in silence they disappeared into the blackness beyond. And the lamps went with them. It was very dark when they had gone, dark and cold.

A little time went by. The children and the dog discovered they were all seated on the ground in a huddle together. The dog licked their noses and sprang to her feet and shook herself: the children climbed painfully to their feet, colder and stiffer than she.

'Nothing fell, look, the way is perfectly clear,' said Josephine at last, softly.

'It's gone,' said Simon, looking back towards the house, 'It's cleared away. Look at the lights.'

The house gleamed through most of its windows at the top of the hill. Many of the trees were gone: the ground was open and terraced.

'It was so dark,' said Josephine, shivering. 'The *darkness* people lived in once: little bits of light and such blackness all round.'

'Let's go back,' said Simon. 'We don't belong here. It might all happen again. We might get caught in it.'

'*Don't*,' said Josephine. Yet the experience over, she felt frightened certainly, but manageably so. She was not near to any kind of panic: she could remember what she had seen and wonder about it.

'Now you see what I meant about the trees,' said Simon, in such a way that it was obvious he felt much the same as Josephine: shaken, yet able to talk.

Something then made them both look at Jason. He stood,

perfectly still, trembling all over. His hands were over his eyes.

'It's all right Jason, it's over,' cried Josephine, taking him by the arm. 'The people have all gone. The trees are all right again.'

'I don't know what you mean, the people, the trees,' cried Jason wildly. 'I saw no people. I didn't notice the trees specially. What do you mean? What happened?'

'But didn't you see the horse and rider, and the branch falling—' began Josephine incredulously.

'I saw *nothing*,' he cried in a kind of howl. 'But I know something horrible happened. I heard the hooves and something rushed by: it was all black and I was so scared, then later things came past again, but I didn't see them. It was horrible, *beastly*.'

'It wasn't exactly horrible this time,' said Simon thoughtfully. He put his arm round Jason and began to walk with him. Josephine followed. They walked up through the garden and as they got nearer and nearer to the house Jason began to recover.

'It was almost as if I'd seen a ghost,' he said suddenly, as they mounted the steps. 'Gosh, Simon, do you think I did? A horrible black something: or was it a dog, or the wind? Goodness, it was scarey for a moment down there!'

When they were at the front door he began to whistle. They pushed it open and came inside, blinking at the light and the black and white tiles of the hall which had been polished that afternoon and shone. The clink of glasses and the sound of carefree, adult voices came from the open door of the sitting room. The smell of alcohol and cigarette smoke enveloped them like a warm, smelly hand across the nostrils.

'Gosh!' said Jason, now almost completely revived. 'I *must* tell Rob this. Bet he's never seen a ghost!'

And he ran up the stairs two at a time.

Simon and Josephine were left looking at one another.

They had to talk about it, but the house seemed to be bursting all over with sound and laughter and too much glaring light.

'The back stairs,' said Simon. 'Nobody uses them.'

He led Josephine upstairs, along a corridor to the head of another steeper flight of steps which led down into the kitchen quarters. It was dark here but they could hear low voices in the kitchen below.

They sat down side by side.

'How perfectly extraordinary,' said Simon at last. 'Jason didn't see anything, hardly. And yet we did, didn't we?'

'And he was *more* frightened because he saw less,' said Josephine slowly. 'And then he forgot being frightened. Or at least he kind of thought himself out of his fear.'

'He couldn't have said that about ghosts and telling Rob if he'd been really frightened then,' agreed Simon. 'Josephine, do you want to tell anybody about what happened?'

Josephine considered. 'No,' she said. 'Or at least not yet.'

'I agree. So you keep your mouth shut and don't blab.'

'I never blab,' said Josephine loftily. She might share experiences with Simon, but he could still irritate her. Yet she realized now with a sense of relief that all her shyness and fear of him had gone. He had been nice to Jason, coming up the garden. He was not too bad, really.

They sat on in silence, feeling the dark about them. It was the kind of comforting half-dark to which one's eyes swiftly adjust.

Josephine looked down towards the streak of light coming from a closed door at the bottom of the stairs and thought suddenly:

She used to sit here a good deal: she used to listen to them in the kitchen. She was less alone that way.

'Simon, have you seen this little girl?' she began, on an impulse. 'She is—well, I think she's one of them.' She shied instinctively from the word Jason had used. 'And I think her name is Margaret. She wears a long nightie; rather a dirty one.'

Simon shot her a quick look. 'Oh yes,' he said, after a pause. 'Of course. She doesn't come out into the garden though.'

'No, she's in the house—' Josephine stopped. He was lying; she was practically certain. He did not want to admit the possibility of her having seen more than he had.

'I only thought I saw her once,' she hastily and untruthfully amended.

'Oh did you? I've seen her, oh, a couple of times,' airily.

Yes, he was lying: had to go one better, always.

'The people outside.' She changed the subject slightly. 'The people outside, I wonder what started them off. What had happened?'

'I know,' he replied rapidly, more sure now of his ground. 'I'll bet that young man on the horse at first was a thief of some kind, galloping off from robbing the house, and the falling tree stopped his getaway and then he was found by the owners of the house coming back from a party and they caught him. I'll bet he was hanged later for his crime, and that's why we saw them like that: you see—people of long ago—when things like that have happened sometimes. If you have eyes to see, like I have. And you have. But Jason hasn't really at all.'

'Maybe it was like that,' said Josephine doubtfully. 'But —I don't know.'

Something was wrong with his theory: though it was neat and did him credit for swift thinking.

'He wasn't carrying anything: any sack of loot,' she said. 'And why did the first woman run like that?'

'To see if her jewellery was safe, of course.'

He was sure and dogmatic.

'I don't think you're right,' said Josephine. She felt very tired, weak and confused all of a sudden.

'Oh, I want my supper. Come on—'

And so they went in search of it without talking any more.

# 6

Hours of sleep and then, in the dark hours of a winter's early morning, another dream, another entry into a short life.

This time she was not Margaret, not at first. From one corner of the room, somewhere near the drawn curtains at the window, she found herself looking down at the body of the child who lay in the bed. A stained dark red satin eiderdown was half on the floor: she lay with only a sheet over her. Her mouth was open, and her breathing was noisy and irregular, a kind of rasping gasp. Her eyes were half open but it didn't seem as if she were focussing on anything. A light shone flickering on her white face, raising great shadows that roamed up and down the hangings and walls and now Josephine could see that two women stood together by the bed holding up a candle, looking at the child and talking together in agitated whispers.

'Holy God, the child's going,' she heard. 'You'll have to answer for your neglect at the Day of Judgement, my girl.'

'Oh, hold your mouth. Who was it wanted my company in the kitchen night after night? Who was it first offered me a drop of something to warm me inside?'

The first woman drew her lips in and remained silent, while the younger one, with the yellow hair, bent over the little girl again and the candle flame wobbled and sent all the shadows reaching and rearing.

'She's awfully sick,' she said with a catch in her voice. 'I ain't never seen her like this before.'

'I tell you the child's dying. Haven't I buried five of my own? Don't you think I know the signs? I wouldn't like to be you when her mamma comes back.'

'Oh, Alice, she may be back this week: I had a letter this morning. I meant to tell you but it slipped my mind. You know how irregular they are, it could all be put off yet again. But Rose and Janet are coming over from the village tomorrow to give a hand with getting the house ready. Oh, Alice, oh, what shall I do? Shall we send Joseph for the doctor? Oh, I'm afraid, Alice. The poor little mite lying here like this: she'd been a bit extra poorly all day but I never thought ... Betty, she said, Betty I can't eat the gruel. I'll just have a drink of water by me, she said. Here you are, my duck I said, and then I went downstairs, never thinking ... Oh Alice, what shall we *do?*'

And the young woman Betty broke into noisy sobs.

Silly fool, thought Josephine, watching her dispassionately. It's no good being sorry now.

Then as she watched the two women who continued talking and drawing the covers up on the recumbent body and uselessly feeling her forehead, she became aware of other sensations: it was as if her awareness had become enriched by having another dimension added to it: now in some way she was joined by the spirit of the child Margaret whose body still lay, just alive, but unconscious, upon the bed. She saw Betty and Alice, especially Betty, as familiar faces she knew; women who had not been actively very un-kind to her but lazy and neglectful and entirely lacking in imagination; and she saw them from a distance as if they were far back down a long dark tunnel and she were near

63

the end, where the light was breaking through and outside was warmth and light and colour unimaginable. But somehow, in spite of the happiness and relief at being so near the tunnel's end, there was also a slight feeling of bewilderment, of disappointment: 'Was that then all? Was that all my life? Aren't I going to have any longer?'

The dream changed: became muddied and muddled as dreams will: Josephine was downstairs with the two women; they stood arguing in the hall with an unkempt youth who picked his nose.

'If the old mare's lame, you'll have to take the young horse, no matter if he's not used to the saddle, and ride as best you know how, Joseph—'

A glimpse outside of a dark windy night; the sound of trees crashing their branches together and groaning and then Josephine somehow found herself in a carriage driving down the avenue towards the house, watching the girl Janey and her husband who now appeared to be Tony Swift in his riding clothes.

'Shall I eat you up?' he said to Janey, taking her by the arm.

'No, it's Christmas and I left my baby behind me,' replied Janey laughing idiotically and then Josephine saw Annabella's Walkie-Talkie doll staggering along down the avenue towards them: 'Mamma, mamma,' it squeaked.

'I hate dolls,' said Josephine loudly and violently, and she woke up.

She was entirely awake, rather cold and though not exactly frightened, troubled in mind. She switched on the torch by her bed and her watch said four o'clock. She very much wanted to reassure herself that her parents slept next door, that all was as it should be, so she got out of bed and put on her dressing gown. As the radiator in her room had remained cold the air outside her warm bed made her shiver. She opened the door and shone her torch and heard the house breathing about her. There was the door of her parents' room and beyond that the big bedroom where the Swifts slept. Miranda and Annabella shared a room beyond that—up three stairs and round a corner was a bathroom and Jason's room, his father's room, Greta's room and the room that had been Janey's who had stayed only two nights. If you continued up the main staircase to the attics you reached the big attic shared by Rupert and Rob, Simon's little room, another bathroom, another empty room which was used as a junk room. That was the house upstairs: nothing sinister, unknown about it.

When Margaret was alone there with Betty and Alice, she must have been the only person on the first floor: the servants would have slept in the attics.

Or would Betty have moved downstairs to be near her? There was so much she did not know. Margaret could not have stood here, with an electric torch to dispel the shadows, a switch to flick on a wall to drive them away entirely. When it was windy there were draughts and draughts could blow candles out altogether, so had Margaret ever stood, quite alone, entirely in the dark?

Josephine, having looked at the door of her parents' room for a moment, decided there was no need to go in and wake them. They were there, she could hear them breathing. After a minute or two, from the room beyond she heard a cough, then a bump and then a heavy footstep. Oh heavens, Tony Swift was coming out.

In one rapid movement Josephine was back inside her room, the door closed. She lay in bed and closed her eyes and tried to sleep. She began to drift, and for no particular reason that she could think of, the face of Tessa Swift now kept coming into her mind. At last she half-slept and it was Tessa's rather deep, emphatic voice she continually heard:

'Oh but you *must* all go on staying with me for ever and ever: I can't be left alone, it isn't good for me,' and while she was saying this she repeatedly twisted her long hair up into a bun and put on her bowler hat. 'I'm going out hunting now, but when I come back *you must all be there*,' she continued with a sidelong, slightly mad look in her eyes.

Seven o'clock: Josephine came to full consciousness again. What *hard* nights one has at Cold Christmas, she thought confusedly. But tomorrow will be the last. What will have happened by then?

For there was more to come, of that she was certain.

# 7

'You know they are really awfully good.'

'Yes, they're going to be most successful. I like this one especially.'

Tony and Tessa Swift were admiring Mrs Palmer's paintings: she had already the preliminary sketches for a couple of different views of the house nearly completed. They stood beside her easel outside on the terrace in the midday sun: it was almost warm. The parts of the garden that lay in shadow were still white with frost but the sun had melted great patches on the lawn so that a bright soft green shone through. Miranda was riding her bicycle about the terrace, followed by Annabella on a tricycle. Josephine sat on a stone balustrade and watched them.

'Where shall we hang it when it's done?' wondered Tony Swift. 'The hall perhaps? Or in our bedroom, Tessa, I can think of a very good place.'

His hand patted his wife's bottom with an affectionate gesture: they looked a very normal contented couple. 'It's extraordinary how dreams can make one go quite wrong about people,' thought Josephine, watching them. 'I might have been quite frightened of Mr and Mrs Swift if I'd never seen them again after my dream last night. They were nasty, somehow. But they're perfectly all right and ordinary now.

In fact, I really don't mind Tony Swift at all, I think I'm getting used to him.'

There was another part of her dream about which she could not say she was mistaken; she knew she was not, but she pushed it very deep down within herself. It was sunny and pleasantly prosaic here in the mid-morning light, nothing to disturb, nothing to fear, one could just take life as it came.

'By the way, darling,' said Tessa, turning to her husband, 'have you finished the children's treasure hunt yet? Placed all the clues?'

'Bill's just putting the finishing touches now. It's as much his hunt as mine, this year. He's thought of some jolly good clues.'

'What's the prize?' asked Josephine.

'The prize is a secret, of course. One should never know what the buried treasure is.'

'Let's get the children all assembled in the hall,' said Tessa. 'We can tell them what to expect and where not to look. Come on girls. See if you can find the others.'

'The boys are all upstairs in Rob's room,' said Josephine. 'I'll go and fetch them, shall I?'

She ran off with a slight anticipation of excitement and pleasure. At last she was beginning to relax and enjoy herself. It would be more satisfactory for them to have something for them all to do together. She resolved to try hard to win the hunt. She was quite quick and good at clues.

'Now,' said Tessa to them all at last assembled in the hall. 'This hunt is a long one and is supposed to take you most of the day : until teatime at least. We are all having a cup of tea together in the sitting room and then there will be a further happening. Tony will read the first clue in a moment to start you off. All the grown-ups' bedrooms are out of bounds as of course is Juan and Isabella's flat. The

68

sitting room is out of bounds too. But apart from that you have the whole house. Greta and Annabella are going to work together: otherwise you're all on your own. Put back any clue you find—they are all written on pieces of paper—so that others coming after you can find it too. Understood? Right, over to you, Tony.'

'The first clue is an easy one thought out by myself,' said Tony. 'Bill here is brainier than me and he thought of all the best rhymes and ideas. But here's an easy one to start you off.

> 'Search within a deep armchair
> You'll find me hiding in my lair.'

'*Not* the sitting room!' he bawled after Rupert, Rob and Jason who had instinctively turned towards the likeliest place to find armchairs.

In the meantime Josephine and Simon with Miranda hard on their heels had turned and made for the billiard room where there were a couple of old armchairs at one end near the television. Simon found the clue first but Josephine was so close she was able to read it over his shoulder:

> 'A little house
> A tiny room
> Within a cupboard
> Behind a broom
> very small indeed am I',

she read.

This halted her and Simon in their tracks a moment and they stood and glared at each other. Josephine realized that she very much wanted to beat Simon in this hunt, to beat them all. But temporarily she was confused: this was a big house rather than a little one or did the Swifts think it was a little house because they were used to even bigger mansions? Were there any tiny rooms apart from lavatories here? Did they mean the broom cupboard?

It was Miranda coming up behind them reading the clue and then running off with a look of triumph that spurred Josephine onto action. After all, Miranda knew the house well. She would follow her.

She followed Miranda to the playroom where of course stood her dolls' house. Already Miranda had the front off and was burrowing inside. Together behind the minute broom in the kitchen they found a scrap of paper with a very short clue upon it as there was room for no more:

'ABC
There I be'

Now Simon was behind them again: the three of them were acting together, whether they wanted to or no.

'Oh bother! I don't know what this means,' wailed Miranda. 'Our letter bricks perhaps. But I don't know where they are.'

Some time went by while they were searching and the room began to fill with some of the others. Then Josephine had a stroke of luck: quite by chance she found herself alone near a bookshelf with some very babyish books, obviously belonging to Annabella. One had ABC in large letters on its cover. She was able to abstract the clue which lay within the first page and return it without anybody else seeing her, and race out of the room on her own.

Time went on. There was clue after clue. The children began to space themselves out and take rests when their concentration waned. Miranda went off to grumble at her mother about something she thought was unfair. Greta and Annabella, hand in hand, very slowly found a few clues and then more or less gave up and Greta settled in the playroom and began to read Annabella a story. It was obvious that the two of them were very happy and contented together and to a certain extent led their own life, apart from the rest of the family.

Shortly before the gong sounded for lunch and a truce was announced, Josephine found herself alone on the back staircase. She was ahead of all the others now and counted as she went:

'Eight steps up
Two steps down
Tucked out of sight
and wrapped in brown'

Her fingers slid about under the stair carpet and she thought, quite casually, of Margaret. This had been one of the places where she had often sat, as Josephine had realized the previous evening. But she had never *seen* her here. She had not, in fact, seen her, other than in dreams for more than a day. Would she not see her again? Her heart began to beat.

'Come, Margaret, please come again,' she said softly. 'Come on. I'm your friend.'

Silence: nothing. Nobody was there. Could Margaret only appear to her when she was not thinking about her particularly?

'Margaret? Aren't I going to see you again?'

Perhaps she was not. Perhaps it was all over. But as she was thinking this, quite of its own accord her heart began to pound again and she began to tremble.

She pushed her fingers further along and found a piece of brown paper just as the gong went.

A nice hot lunch would stop the trembling and the excitement for a while.


In the long hours of the afternoon, Josephine and Simon met one another in the hall. The others were all upstairs. Josephine stopped counting the tiles which had been her occupation and stared at Simon because he was pulling an extra sweater over his head as if he were going out.

'You've not finished the hunt?' she asked incredulously.

'Oh, I'm fed up with the silly hunt. They don't do the clues well enough. I've a much better idea.'

'Whatever do you mean?'

'I'm on a treasure hunt outside,' he said mysteriously.

'Outside? But there's nothing outside. Tessa said it would be in the house.'

'It's nothing to do with the childish treasure hunt today, don't you understand? It's outside you'll find the really important stuff. I'll bet something got dropped.'

'Simon, you mean, what we saw last night,' said Josephine slowly, beginning to understand. 'You still think it really was a thief and in his fall he'd have dropped some money or something? But Simon, you've got it all wrong. I'm sure about that now. And anyway, it was so long ago. More than a hundred years I should think. Perhaps two. If anything had been dropped it wouldn't be left lying around now.'

'Nonsense, things can be found *hundreds* of years later,' shouted Simon, slamming the door.

'Yes, but anyway you're wrong—' began Josephine. She made a movement towards the door as if to explain it all to him, but it had shut in her face.

'Oh well. *Go* and look outside then. I bet you wouldn't have given up if you hadn't been at least two clues behind me,' she said, though only to herself, and then turned her attention to:

'A game of chess
    You could play here
From the opening of the door
    Count one, two, three
And then count four'

Right. She was at the front door looking at the black and white tiles. One two three and then four made seven. She counted seven and stared about her. Nothing to see. Did it mean black only, or white only? She began to work it out when Rob and Rupert appeared. They were working together. 'Come on, Rupert, start counting the stairs,' Josephine heard Rob say. She could hardly resist a superior smile. They were as far behind as *that*, were they? And on the wrong stairs too.

But it was nice of Rob to help his younger brother: though he bossed and shouted at him they were obviously good friends really: perhaps they needed to stick together with their parents so much away.

Rupert began to count and Josephine, fearing nothing from such slow, steady plodders said to Rob,

'You're on the wrong staircase, you know.'

'Are we? Right. Come on, Rupe. The back stairs.'

Imperturbable, a good though rather lethargic general, he directed his troops elsewhere.

Meanwhile Josephine worked it out every way in the hall and was stuck. No way of counting seemed to bring her closer to the hidden clue. But after about five minutes she saw the pleasant, lively little man, Bill, whose surname she didn't know but who was Jason's father, coming downstairs and she appealed to him.

'Are you sure you put this one in the hall in the right place?'

'Oh, you're up as far as that,' he said, smiling at her. 'You're getting on very nicely. Let me see. It might be a bit difficult to spot. But if I help you I'll have to help the others. Look at the seventh tile.'

'But I've done that.'

'Have you looked really closely?'

Josephine bent down again. The seventh tile was white

73

and for the first time she noticed a piece of white shiny paper was stuck on to it. It was really very unnoticeable. But you could peel it off and on its other side was written—

'Thanks very much,' she said.

'Let's stick it back on. I've got it a bit crooked now so it should be easier to see.'

She went upstairs, repeating softly to herself:

> 'Under some stout old drawers I lie
> Seeing what dust I can espy.'

That should be easy enough. There should be some chests of drawers about the place. Then she remembered that all the adults' bedrooms were out of bounds and that her own room had only a wardrobe. She began to look in the other, upstairs rooms. In Jason's room she found Jason lying on his bed reading a comic.

'Have you given up?' she asked.

'Not exactly,' he yawned. 'I got stuck and so I came in here for a little rest.'

'Oh Jason! Let me help you.'

'All right,' he said, sitting up and quite agreeable to be started off again.

'What was the clue?' asked Josephine with a pleasant feeling of superiority.

'The chess one, they don't seem to have a chess board anywhere in this house. I looked all over the playroom and the junk room and then got fed up.'

'Oh but Jason—' Josephine stopped. She had not realized he was so near behind her or she would not have given her offer of help so blithely. And how silly of him not to have thought of the hall, especially with that bit about the door.

> 'From the opening of the door
> Count one, two, three
> And then count four'

74

She quoted it to him. 'Of course it isn't a proper board. How could a board have a door?'

'I dunno. Didn't seem to make sense, that bit. *Oh*—' light slowly began to dawn upon him and his mouth fell open. 'It's extraordinary how stupid one can look when one's brain is working,' thought Josephine.

'*Oh*, you mean the hall: the black and white tiles,' he said at last. 'What a stupid idiot I've been.'

He stood up, looking rumpled but alert, and Josephine realized she had a rival in him to fear. She had underrated him.

'Before you go down you can just tell me something,' she said rapidly. 'What's in the junk room anyway?'

'Oh, old tennis racquets and books and stacks of pictures and a chest or so and some wooden chairs,' he told her. 'Why?'

'Just wondered.'

Jason ran down to the hall while Josephine made for the junk room into which she had not previously penetrated. It was a largish corner room with two windows, one above the front door looking over the gravelled drive, the other facing west over the main part of the garden. This window was above and a little to the side of Josephine's own bedroom window. The junk room should have been a pleasant room. With its two windows it was light and airy and it had interesting corners piled with things like old sewing machines and ironing boards and wooden chairs and an ancient croquet set. There were piles of dusty books, one or two pictures with broken frames and there was an old chest of drawers. The room smelt of dust and old things but not unpleasantly so.

Yet there was something here which Josephine did not like. She walked in, knocking over a pile of books as she did so, and as she went to pick them up and felt the thick quiet of the room, she had a renewed awareness of the child who had lived so much of her life alone in the rooms and corridors of this house: of the weight of long winter afternoons such as this when time seemed to be measured by a creak, a sigh, as much as by the slow tick of a clock. If boredom sometimes laid its own suffocating evil-smelling blanket around Josephine's own shoulders—what had it not done to Margaret, neglected and forgotten as she had been? Had Margaret once poked about in this dreary room, wondering what to do?

*No*: Josephine opened an old book and stared sightlessly at it. No: this had been *Alice's* room in Margaret's time. The room of Alice, the cook.

And now Josephine saw with the inner eye of her imagination how it had been. She knew she was imagining: making up, and yet it seemed so right. She was Margaret, by the door, looking in one afternoon and there was Alice by a wardrobe which stood against the wall, *there*. The bed would have been opposite. There was a chair, a jug and basin, a big black trunk.

Alice was changing her clothes; her old blue dress, stained under the arms, was across a chair: she stood in an old, yellowish bodice and petticoat.

'May I come in?' Margaret had said.

'No, child, you may not. Get back to your room, you have no business here.'

And Alice would have come across the room, stern and hard, and slammed the door in Margaret's face. The room would have smelt of her. Had Margaret minded? Would she have wanted to see what lay in Alice's big, black box?

Why had she thought of this box so strongly? There was nothing resembling such a thing in the room now. Yet Josephine felt sure that the cook, Alice, who had buried five, had possessed a big black box like a coffin.

A black beetle ran across the floor.

'Ugh!' Josephine shuddered away from it and went quickly over to the chest of drawers in the corner of the room. Yes, you could see where the dust underneath had been disturbed by something pushed underneath. She pulled out the piece of paper and held it to the light, which was rapidly waning. The sun had been altogether swallowed by thick clouds and the afternoon was nearly over. It was very quiet and all the objects in the junk room began to give out the distinct miasma of objects seldom visited: a kind of quiet self-assertion; here we are, here we have stood for years, we will live longer than you, some of us. If you don't turn your head we can move, whisper, do what we were doing when you interrupted us—

A footstep suddenly behind her, a cold hand on her neck.

'Aie!' squealed Josephine. Jason, whose hand it had been, roared with laughter.

'Oh, you are a beast,' she said weakly.

'I know I'm a beast, but you looked so funny! Come on, is that a clue you've just found? I've caught you up, you see.'

'Oh bother you. I shouldn't have helped you like that. And how did you find the paper in the hall so easily?'

'I didn't see it absolutely right away, but Tony was going to ring the gong for tea in a minute and make us all stop, so he helped me find it. He's given me just three minutes to get the last clue, so come on, let's see it.'

'It's not fair!' cried Josephine. 'I was here first!'

'Oh, you girls are always saying something isn't fair. Miranda is all screechy about an earlier clue and says she won't do any more. She's given up completely.'

'Oh well. The last one's a bit of a cheat anyway,' said

Josephine, reluctantly showing it to him.

The last clue read:

> 'When sun is set
>   And tea is et
> A visitor from long ago
>   Will point it out
> (Don't scream or shout)
> Just follow the pointing finger!'

'What on earth is going to happen, I wonder?'

'Oh, I should think Tony Swift will dress up as something or other,' said Jason in a rather patronizing voice. 'It's the kind of thing he likes to do, you know.'

As the gong sounded to summon them to tea Josephine looked out of the window.

'There's Simon coming back up the garden,' she said, 'he'll just be in time.'

He walked with his hands hunched in his pockets, looking cold and cross. It certainly was not the look of someone who has found whatever he was looking for.

# 8

Downstairs the lights were being switched on and the curtains drawn. It had changed from afternoon to evening.

'Come on, everybody,' cried Tessa at the door of the sitting room. 'We're all having tea in here. Come and sit by this little table, Jason and Josephine. Simon, you can make yourself useful and pass round the teacups. Where are Rob and Rupert? Oh there they are. Never mind if you haven't finished the clues. You'll have a chance to catch up later, though it would be helpful to have the last clue.'

'Josephine and I have done it all,' said Jason.

'Jolly good. Just sit down and have a sandwich now, will you?'

As they ate, Josephine could see that everybody was in the room, eating, even little Annabella and Greta. Annabella had her Walkie Talkie doll with her and was trying to feed it pieces of cake.

Mrs Palmer sat on the sofa, being polite and brightly conversational.

'Well, you *have* kept the children well amused this afternoon. What a splendid idea and how clever of Tony and Bill. I'm sure I could never have thought up all those clues. It's been fun, hasn't it, Josephine?'

Josephine, prodded into conversation in this wise, replied

briefly but rather tonelessly 'yes' and stuffed her mouth with biscuit so that she wouldn't have to say any more. She had enjoyed the early part of the hunt but now was feeling weary of it, yet keyed up and uneasy at the same time. Really, now she came to think of it, she was feeling rather peculiar altogether. Perhaps she was not well? Perhaps she was sickening for something. Her stomach felt apprehensive and a tight band of something seemed to be constricting the top of her head.

Tea seemed to drag on interminably but at last Tessa began to collect the cups and saucers and pile them on a trolley which was wheeled from the room. People milled in and out for a few moments, helping, and then Tessa turned out all the lights apart from a light under a big oil painting that stood opposite the fireplace. It was a painting of a woodcutter's hut in the middle of a snowy forest which Josephine had not noticed before.

Her mother and father admired it and then somehow, to Josephine's continued unease, the grown-ups' conversation changed from pictures and art to talking about ghosts. She heard Tessa saying that there were no ghosts at Cold Christmas, although she had once heard a story of a man in a dark cloak and boots being seen crossing the hall—

And so saying she switched the light under the picture out and they sat in firelight for about a second. And then a kind of greenish muffled light appeared through the half open door and the tall figure of a man strode in, his cloak falling dramatically from his outstretched arm— his gauntleted finger pointing across the room.

Miranda produced a very satisfactory shriek and Annabella hid her face in Greta's lap.

Josephine sat, stricken. The man was the half-drunken gentleman who had stumbled from the carriage: he was Margaret's father. She could not move for a moment.

There had been an instant's silence. Then Jason, at Josephine's side, broke it.

'The pointing finger!' he shouted. 'The last clue said follow the pointing finger!'

Instantly the lights all went on and Tony Swift was revealed, dressed up in a cloak and boots and with some sort of white make-up on his face pointing across the room to the grandfather clock in the far corner.

Jason sprang to his feet but Rupert, who had not reached the last clue but had been quick on the uptake, was a little before him. He raced to the clock and triumphantly pulled out a brown paper parcel from behind it and everybody laughed and clapped.

'Oh blast it: I gave it away nicely, didn't I?' Josephine heard the disgruntled Jason muttering to himself.

Now everybody was talking and moving about and congratulating Tony Swift on his costume and on the surprise.

'Is there really a story of a cloaked gentleman ghost connected with this house?' Josephine heard her father ask.

'No, there's nothing like that at all, or at least that I've ever heard of,' replied Tessa Swift, laughing. 'I just put it in to add to the atmosphere and because Tony had the costume ready.'

'It will be used within the next few weeks when we start shooting,' said Jason's father. 'It's a good cloak, isn't it? Suits him.'

'Ah, they knew how to dress in the old days,' said Tony Swift, taking the cloak off and revealing his usual jersey and trousers underneath. 'And now let's see what you got, Rupert old boy. The prize was Tessa's department, not mine.'

Rupert tore at the paper. 'It's a book,' he said, holding it up. 'A nice big one.'

The book had a splendid picture of galloping horses on the cover, and its title was *Horses, Horses and More Horses*.

'Oo lovely,' said everybody except Josephine, who knew she would have been the person to have most appreciated this treasure. It was maddening to have it won by Rupert, who although he was looking quite pleased, would obviously have preferred a book called *Aeroplanes, Aeroplanes and More Aeroplanes* or *Cars, Cars and More Cars*. In fact, all the boys probably would have preferred something like that. It was a prize which should have been won by herself or Miranda. What a waste! In some way it was typical of Tessa Swift to have chosen a prize like that and for the wrong person to have won it, thought Josephine bitterly.

She was not the only one to feel a little put out: it was evident that Rob was somewhat resenting his little brother's success, especially as Rupert, now turning somersaults upon the sofa, had caught him a blow across the face with his foot.

'Look out, you silly twit,' he exclaimed angrily and then said loudly, 'anyway I don't think you were a very good ghost, Uncle Tony. You didn't fool *me*. You're quite on the wrong track anyway. What about Jason's ghost then, down the garden? He really *did* see something, didn't you, Jason?'

His voice rang out and he had everybody's attention.

'What's that?' said Tony Swift instantly.

'Yes, what's that?' echoed Tessa. 'A *real* ghost! But how exciting! Why didn't you tell us all, Jason?'

Jason looked uneasy. 'Oh well,' he muttered, glancing at Simon. 'Perhaps it was nothing much, but the others saw more than I did.'

He stopped, and said no more. But he had gone rather pale and Josephine saw Tessa noticing this.

'Come on,' she said cheerfully and relentlessly. 'I want

to hear more of this. Who were the others? You, Simon?'

Simon looked furiously at Jason and then at his aunt.

'We thought there was something in the oak avenue,' he said at last. 'But we could have been wrong. It was dark and a bit spooky.'

'But this is simply fascinating. What on earth did you see?'

'A rider or something,' put in Jason, as Simon was obviously not going to speak and Josephine sat silent. 'I definitely heard galloping hooves. And so did Susie.'

He patted the dog who lay at his feet. 'She shivered all over and crouched to the ground,' he said. 'She didn't like it at all.'

'How odd. Dogs are supposed to have a very quick sense of something out of the ordinary. At what sort of time were these hoof beats, then?'

'About now, I suppose,' answered Jason. 'After tea when it was dark but not too late.'

'Come on, Tessa,' said her husband. 'Let's go ghost hunting. Anybody else like to come? Are you psychic, Bill? Don? Let's waken all the spirits! If we can't get the beasts to utter on Christmas Eve, perhaps we can raise a nice eerie shriek or two, or a rattle of chains.'

Then Josephine, who during this conversation had been feeling more and more uneasy, backed to the window, drew aside the curtain and looked out. There was an unfamiliar blue and white look.

'It's snowing!' she exclaimed.

And now there was no stopping them. Everybody, except her mother and Greta, both of whom shivered and held out their hands to the fire, was bent on going out, the men as much as the children.

'My boots, Daddy!' shrieked Annabella, clutching her

83

doll tightly to her. 'Get me my boots. Rosamund hasn't seen any snow yet. She must come too!'

And so, after a wild scurry of putting on garments in the hall, they were outside in the dusk where a thin powder of snow already lay on the gravel and stone-flagged terrace, and in the two big urns and down over the lawn and on the bushes and trees. It was lighter, easier to see, than it had been; the snow had done this. It had lessened already, and only an occasional flake drifted down.

Before she was aware what was happening Josephine found herself being swept along with them all, down the first little flight of steps, past the pond and the ornamental hollies to the lower lawn, and then down again.

She ached all over and felt dreadful; everything was building up together and she could not stop it, and she knew, knew without any question that what they were doing was bad, dangerous, was leading to something, some disaster, she knew not what.

She caught at Simon's arm.

'Can't we stop them? They mustn't go down like this. It's all wrong.'

'I know it is. Stupid Jason, can't he have kept his big mouth shut? He didn't understand. They none of them do.'

'Don't let's go!' called Josephine vainly, but Rob, together with his uncle and aunt were far ahead. Tony Swift was giving his little daughter Annabella a piggyback. Tessa was holding a big torch which she kept flicking on and off. Miranda, Rupert and Jason were a little behind them. On a rather different course of their own walked Josephine and Jason's fathers talking away together.

'I say, Susie, come here, girl, come here, it's all right.'

Tessa's voice floated back to them and half a second later Susie herself appeared, running back towards the house, her tail clamped down tight to her woolly behind.

They caught up with the rest of the party then, and all bunched together, calling Susie in vain. But she did not come.

'That *is* odd,' Tessa Swift said thoughtfully. 'She's never done that before. She was running ahead quite happily and then we turned down to go over the rough grass and she halted dead and then bolted. You know, I'm beginning to believe you, Jason. I think certainly that something or someone must have frightened her down here. Let's go on a bit.'

'Oo Daddy, do let me down,' wriggled Annabella. 'I want Rosamund to walk between the trees.'

And so they all wandered about in the beginning part of the oak avenue, walking a little further, and pausing, and listening and chatting, and the dreadful feeling tightened and tightened inside Josephine.

Margaret was nothing but good, she knew: but there had been other forces raised within the last few days that had been far from good: there had been hunting, of various kinds, desperation, injury, death, even if only the death of animals. Something had been unleashed: there was a building up of tension that could only be released by something else happening.

She was near to Annabella and her doll, Annabella was bent over, walking her doll up a great tree root, and a memory connected with this doll flashed into Josephine's mind: it was when her dream had gone all nightmarish and muddled and she had seen the doll walking by itself with stilted stiff-legged strides up between the trees saying 'Mamma, Mamma!'

And then Margaret finally broke through to her as if from a great distance and as if she had been trying for a long time, and Josephine realized why she had felt so ill at ease. She had had her mind too full of other things and had not listened, but now at last she saw the face of Margaret imploring, anxious, appear at her side and she was conscious of her, moving between herself and Annabella and looking upward and then back into Josephine's face, and then upward towards the treetops again where the high branches stood, whitened on one side with snow. Her lips moved as if she were desperately trying to shout, but no sound came.

Just as the wild gust of wind blew into her face Josephine reached the startled Annabella, snow beat in her face as she picked her up, and as she moved away she saw, as if in slow motion, the whole of the top of the large oak tree crack, hang above them and fall with a shattering thud and series of lesser thuds to the ground.

Nobody was hurt. Josephine and Annabella were surrounded by a mass of twigs which did not touch them, but the heaviest part of the split trunk had landed where Annabella had been only a second previously.

There was an instant's complete, shocked silence.

Then Annabella began to cry: 'My doll, my doll, Rosamund!'

Tony and Tessa Swift came running up calling to Annabella and Tony picked her up, but she continued to struggle and cry and point towards the fallen tree trunk underneath which Tessa's big torch showed up a piece of material and what looked like some hair.

Tony wrenched at it for a moment.

'I'm sorry, Annabella,' he said at last. 'Your doll's smashed to smithereens. But thank goodness it was nothing worse than that.'

'Cor!' cried Rob and Rupert, running up now and jostling each other to look. 'What a smash!'

Everybody began talking all together and Rob wrenched at the tree trunk, finally succeeding in pulling off the doll's head, though the body lay underneath heavy wood, hopelessly crushed and mangled.

'I'm afraid her eyes have gone, too,' he said, ruefully. 'They're all squinty.'

Annabella's cries not surprisingly redoubled at being handed these grisly remains and she was picked up by Tony again while Josephine's own father ran up to her and put his arm round her. 'Are *you* all right?' he said. 'Sure nothing got you?'

'My goodness Josephine; we must be grateful to you.' Now Tessa was speaking to her in a rather shaky voice. 'I didn't see quite what happened, but if you hadn't chanced to pick Annabella up like that she could have been killed. And you could have been killed too. However did you see that tree coming down on you in time?'

'I just did,' said Josephine.

'We owe you a very big debt of thanks then,' said Tony Swift. 'It looks to me very much as if you've saved her life. Come on, everybody. Let's go home. I don't like these beastly snow flurries. We'll dry out indoors and have a drink and thank Josephine properly. Bloody unsafe those oak trees! That one must have been partially hollow. I feel inclined to have the whole lot of them down.'

'You mustn't do that,' said Simon at his side. 'It's over now. Nothing more will fall.' He looked at Josephine, but she said nothing. Yet she experienced a great feeling of lightness and freedom: as if something oppressive and evil had lifted, had gone.

It was as they were trudging back that she realized Margaret had gone too. Had she gone for ever?

'We are now past the Shortest Day and the Year is

drawing to its close,' wrote Josephine in her diary. That was good; she liked the way the words rang out. 'The Year is drawing to its close': yes. The Old Year, dying. She drew the blankets luxuriously around her, curled further down her bed and yawned. A lot had happened today but it would be difficult to get it all down. It was not every day that one saved somebody's life. They had made a lot of fuss about that: she had been quite the heroine of the evening. Only Annabella was not particularly grateful; she seemed to think that Josephine might have saved her doll too while she was about it. Lucky, spoilt Annabella: already her father had promised her a new one. However—to work—

'Today I saved a child's life,' wrote Josephine. 'It happened like this ...' She looked at the two lines left for that date and sighed. They did not give one much room to spread oneself, these people who made diaries.

'A great tree fell,' she wrote and stopped again. There was no point in writing more: it wasn't as if she were ever likely to forget.

She paused again and yawned. She felt so tired, and truth to tell, rather cross and weepy.

'Over-excited,' her mother had said about half an hour ago and had sent her to bed early but she had not minded.

'The Old Year is dying'; the very phrase brought tears to her eyes now, for some reason.

'This is the most extraordinary place,' she wrote next, coming over into the space for the next day. 'And I have felt most extraordinary.'

And now she had repeated the same word twice, which was bad. Really this writing business was very hard work; thank goodness she had nearly finished the year. Only four days more to go. She would not bother with a diary next year, too much effort. She would finish off now, in fact— nothing else much could possibly happen.

'The Year has ended, nothing more has happened,' she scrawled defiantly across the last four days. There, done! Now she could go to sleep.

Nothing more had *better* happen, or it would spoil her diary.

# 9

'Simon? Are you awake? May I come in?'

Josephine half opened Simon's bedroom door and peeped in. It was after eight; he ought to be awake, or dressing.

He was sitting up in bed reading a science fiction magazine. Carefully arranged beside him were a pile of books, two apples and a bag of toffee. On a chair on the other side of his bed were a chessboard, a model aeroplane, a transitor radio and a glass of water. It looked as if he were prepared for everything a boy might happen to need in bed.

'Oh it's *you*,' he said ungraciously. 'What do you want? Actually it's not a bad idea, your coming in, because I've found something you ought to read.'

'Oh, all right, Simon. I had to come. Now I'm here I can see I was right. You're in her room. This was *Betty's* room. I can see the balustrade through the window just as I could in my dream. Please tell me, Simon, what did you dream about last night?'

He gazed at her blankly. 'I don't know who you're talking about,' he remarked. 'Who is Betty, anyway? And last night—let me see. School dinners. I dreamt about school dinners.'

'Oh *no*,' said Josephine, disappointed. 'Try again. You

can't just dream about school dinners. Your dream must have had something else in it.'

'I had an especially yucky school dinner,' continued Simon dreamily, 'and then, oh yes, there was more. I was packing something—to go home, I suppose.'

'Yes, yes,' cried Josephine in great excitement. 'That's much better. More. There must have been more.'

'I don't know what you're *on* about. All right, let's think. It was a muddly sort of dream, I was all worried. I had to hurry because—well I suppose the coach was going. I had to get everything in. Now, that's funny. Of course, I wasn't at school by then, come to think of it. I was in this room. But it's such a muddle. I was putting in stuff like spoons and candlesticks. Then I thought I was moving house. I began to drag a wardrobe along too. It was ridiculous. I think I woke up then.'

'Dragging something—hurrying—packing in this room,' cried Josephine even more excitedly. 'Yes, *yes*. We've sort of shared a dream. I thought we might, as you're in her room.'

'Am I going potty or you?' asked Simon, getting out of bed and stretching. 'In whose room for heaven's sake? I thought this little girl you saw was called Margaret, not Betty? I was going to show you something that could have been about her, too.'

'Later, later,' cried Josephine, walking up and down the room. 'I must tell you about Betty, and Alice and my dream. It was so frantic, and you've gone and had some of it too!'

While Simon put on his jeans and jersey and laced up his shoes, before she drew a deep breath and began, she thought back over the events of the night, her last dream at Cold Christmas.

It was the least clear of her dreams, but the urgency and

worry had made it the strongest and in some ways the most unpleasant.

She had been packing in Simon's little room. She had been Betty: stricken with the full knowledge of what she had let happen, frantic that the parents were returning, desperate to get out of the house. She had seen the lights of the approaching carriage down the avenue, knew there was some accident or delay, but not how much time she had. She flung dresses, underclothes, bonnets, pell mell on top of one another into her wooden box, open upon the bed. There were other things too, snatched up in her hurry, which she wrapped in her underclothes and nightgown. Through her head coursed a continual inner monologue which ran something like this:

'They're coming, they're coming, she'll find her, I can't stand it, I must be gone, the back stairs—as they come up the front I go down the back. How can I manage my box? It's so heavy—I'll pull it down—hide it perhaps in a shed —two of Rose's boys can fetch it later for a sixpence—my wages that are due—I'll have to leave them—just as well I've a little something to make up—they owe it to me really—no one to speak for me—never mind, I can get a position as a maidservant, no nursemaiding again for me. Oh, the poor little thing! Hush, don't think of her. Oh, they're coming, they're coming!'

Then there was a further confusion of sensations, the heavy box bumping behind her down the uncarpeted stairs, the drag along the passage, the darkness, rain and wind of the night outside. Her legs could hardly move, she was dragging a ton weight. It was the worst of all the worry dreams she had ever had and it woke her up.

'My word, that's pretty fantastic,' said Simon when she had told him a little more of her dreams about Margaret and about Betty and Alice. 'It's *fantastic* to share a dream like that. It's not been a dream really. It's something more, isn't it? Here—you must read what I found in an old book that had been knocked over by someone in the junk room. I was just poking about in there last night before going to bed. It's a book of true ghost stories collected by some old chap or other way back and this story *fits*. It fits more than I realized. Start here.'

He handed an old dusty-smelling book to Josephine and pointed to a page, but first of all she turned back to look at the frontispiece of the book. It said:

*True Tales of Ghostly Visitations and Hauntings in*
*the Southern Counties of England*
compiled by Samuel Shorter

The date of publication was 1863.

'Oh come on, come on,' said Simon impatiently. 'It's just an old book. I don't think the people before Tessa and Tony had moved all their stuff out: they just left it in the room. Most of the stories are very dull, really. It wasn't until I'd read several others that I came upon this one. Do *read* it, if you can read, that is.'

'Don't be ridiculous,' replied Josephine coldly. She began forthwith:

One of the most touching accounts of a child ghost came to my ears only the other day. It concerns a little girl, Margaret C—— who, in the concluding years of the last century resided in a country house which I shall call Colesworth Park, although that is not its name, in the Northern part of the county of H————shire. The ghost of this child has been seen on several occasions and has appeared only to another child, never having been seen by a grown person.

'There you are!' cried Josephine excitedly, 'yes, that's right!'

The true account of little Margaret C—— was given me by a Mrs Barker, now past the age of sixty, who has lived in a village nearby to Colesworth Park and for the last ten years has kept the village shop. When a young girl of some ten or eleven years, she recollects helping her mother, who was then resident as housekeeper in the house, to polish the silver and wash some of the china. She was a careful and painstaking girl and so often entrusted with this task. She recollects, as if it were yesterday, several times encountering a strange child, dressed only in a white cotton nightgown, upon the back stairs and occasionally along the upstairs corridors of the house. The child would smile at her and sometimes seem as if about to speak, but eventually always ran away. Mrs Barker was in those days a sturdy matter-of-fact girl and she soon came to the conclusion that this child could only be a spirit from another world, but was not in the least frightened or upset by her, mentioning her on more than one occasion to her mother and to the other servants. She was laughed at and ridiculed as none of them ever saw or heard the child and so after a while she held her peace, not wanting to appear too fanciful and foolish.

Years later, when her mother was no longer in employment at the big house, and she herself had married and was living in the village, she was greatly interested to hear, through a friend of hers who was then a housemaid at Colesworth Park, of another reappearance of the selfsame child spirit; again to a girl of some eleven years, who on this occasion was staying as a guest in the house together with her mother and older sister.

This young girl had fallen ill of a fever and had been confined to bed for several days. One evening she was startled to see a strange child leaning over her bed and looking at her, as if she were sorry she were ill and wanted to make friends with her. Half thinking she had dreamt, she at first said nothing to her mother, but when she saw the child again, the next evening at the same time, appear quite suddenly by her bedside she called her sister, who happened to be just outside the door. Upon the sister's entrance the child apparition ran hastily out of the door, passing the older girl but entirely unseen by her, although she was bearing a candle in her hand and the room was already well lit.

'Oh where has she gone?' cried the younger sister, in distress at seeing the apparition vanish. 'You bad girl, you have startled her and she did so want to make friends—'

'That is hardly a kind thing to say when you called me in yourself,' retorted the older sister. 'And in any case I don't know to whom you are referring. I startled nobody: you were quite alone.'

This time, because both the mother and the older sister were of a speculative, talkative disposition, the story of a child haunting the upper passages and rooms of the house was not laughed at, but given some belief and this is how the occurrence reached the ears of Mrs Barker's friend and soon of Mrs Barker herself. Mrs Barker was not slow to communicate her own experiences in the house at a similar age and her story led the owner of the house, a Mrs Ramsey by name, to make a little enquiry as to the families who had occupied it before her.

After some research into parish records, for the house had changed hands many times, she found that in the year 1797 a child, Margaret C——, aged seven years and six months, had died in the house. By making further enquiries among the elderly folk residing in the neighbourhood, she was finally able to discover that this child had been the only child of a rich and spendthrift young couple who had made a great fuss of her as a baby but gradually, finding themselves with no further offspring, had abandoned her more and more to the care of servants while they had enjoyed themselves in their house in London. The husband was both a drunkard and a gambler, the wife a very pretty woman, who had her head turned by countless admirers. They grew to think less and less about how their child was faring, and when she caught a bad chill and it turned to a putrid fever they knew nothing of it, as they were as usual, from home. Returning at last they found the poor neglected child lying dead in her bed; the nursemaid run away and several articles of value missing from the house. The young mother was inconsolable for a time, but eventually she and her husband returned to their profligate life in London and before a year was out had gambled away all their wealth and so the house was sold; the couple left the county and nothing more was heard of them.

Mrs Barker tells me that Mrs Ramsey was much interested in this little tale; and, curious as to why the spirit of the child had returned, resolved to introduce other young girls as guests in the house and see if further contact with little Margaret C—— could be made: however her project met with no success and within a couple of years Mrs Ramsey herself had died and the house was sold again. If there were other sightings of Margaret C—— Mrs Barker did not hear of them, and so the matter rests but for one interesting story, which after a little hesitation Mrs Barker related to me. I shall let her speak in her own words.

'As you see, sir, I have kept this little shop for the last ten years and past and very pleasant and useful employment it gives me. You can imagine that in a small place like this I know all my customers very well, but from time to time a stranger walks in, as happened only the other week. On this occasion it was a pleasant woman in her fifties who informed me that her husband had just found employment working for Farmer X and that consequently she and her family which consisted of herself, her husband, her son, and her elderly father of over eighty years had come to live within the Parish boundaries. There being nobody else in the shop we fell to talking and among other things she told me that although this village was strange to herself and her husband her father had known it well as a lad, having been employed at Colesworth Park, until he met with an accident from which he has been lame to this very day. "But he often speaks of his boyhood here," she went on to say, "and his years of working at the Park: there was some sort of tragedy while he was there I believe, a child died of neglect and soon afterwards the place was sold up. I've heard too that since those days the Park and gardens have been much altered for the better, a great many old trees cut down and it looks quite different to what it did in Father's day. Poor Father! He feels a kind of remorse yet for what happened, though it was none of his fault and even if he had not been knocked from his horse while fetching the doctor the child would have died in any case. But he says that is not all of it."

'Why, how do you mean?' I answered her with a lively curiosity, as you can imagine.

Josephine had been reading so quickly that she became a little confused here as to who was talking, turned back a page to find it was Mrs Barker, the owner of the post office who had seen Margaret when she was a girl—and was further interrupted by Simon's saying impatiently 'Come on, hurry up. Where have you got to?'

'You see, you were all wrong about there being a thief. It was Joseph going for the doctor,' she could not help exclaiming. 'It's just as I dreamt. I saw Joseph in the hall, with Alice and Betty, and they were telling him to ride for the doctor.'

'All right, all right,' Simon said grudgingly. 'But buck up and finish it, do.'

She turned back to the book, back to this account which had been written over a hundred years ago, describing events yet further away in time, and plunged into the story again.

' " He was only a boy at the time, not eighteen, and I tell him repeatedly that he could not be blamed but he will go on that he could have been kinder to the little girl who died. He was employed as a gardener's boy and stable boy and apparently she lacked companions of any kind and used to pester him to play with her and to give her a ride on the cart horse and to talk to her. She used to lie in wait for him and watch him sweep out the stable yard and chatter nineteen to the dozen to him. He was sorry for her and yet he found her a dreadful nuisance and wished many a time that she would go away and leave him alone.

' "One day I think she had been more persistent than usual and followed him everywhere and teased him constantly with the question: Will you be my true friend, Joseph? and at last he turned on her and cried out no, he would not and she should seek out little girls of her own age, and she looked at him as if she were stricken to the heart and went away without a word. And he was most upset because he knew very well she could not follow his advice as she never saw any other children. And although she never came near him after that day, he felt sorrier and sorrier about her and began to realize how her maid neglected her. As for her mother, she was away all summer.

' "The warm days passed and the winter crept on, and he hardly saw her except at a window until the day came when she was dying and he was sent on horseback for the doctor and had the accident from which he has been lame to this day. And he's never been able to forget the little girl. He's told me about it many and many a time: though for the life of me I don't know what a stable-boy could have done to help such a child. But to look at another side of it, he's been an excellent father to me and my sisters—so good comes out of everything as God is watching us from heaven, that's what I say. And I had better be getting back to him. I mustn't stay here gossiping all afternoon: he's aged a good deal since he's had the pneumonia and the move's unsettled him." And with that she went out of the shop.

'Well, I don't mind telling you, sir, it was this recollection of the little girl I had seen as a spirit child so long ago that brought it all back to me so vividly that the tears streamed from my eyes, and has prompted the tale you have heard today, which is true in every detail. I cannot take you, alas, to the old man Joseph because he died soon after his removal back here. His daughter and her husband still live in the neighbourhood but she cannot add anything further to the little story she told me and a sad little story it is I'm afraid, sir, but there, every child ghost must be a sad ghost in a sense because it's a little life cut short, isn't it, sir?'

When she had finished Josephine sat quite silent. She

wished very much that she had been reading this on her own, without Simon impatiently watching her and waiting to talk about it. Through the old-fashioned words and close print a story had emerged and burnt itself into her heart. She could now see so much, so clearly. And the shattering thing was how closely it proved her own dreams and experiences to have been true.

'Well?' Simon demanded the moment her eyes left the page. 'Isn't it extraordinary? What do you think? *You* started all this going, you know. To be quite honest, I actually didn't quite see this Margaret myself. And I agree, I was wrong about Joseph, thinking he was a thief when he wasn't at all. Yet I did have this quite separate sort of feeling about treasure, something taken away and hidden.'

'That's it!' cried Josephine, suddenly coming to life and in a sense relieved to turn from Margaret to Betty. 'You dreamt that part. Candlesticks and spoons, Simon. I didn't quite get that, just that there was something wrapped. She'd stolen the candlesticks and silver to pay for her wages. The book said something about valuables missing. Suppose she never came back for her box? Couldn't get anybody to fetch it for her? Was too frightened or something?'

'You mean it's *still around somewhere.*'

'Why not?' cried Josephine recklessly. 'I was right over the other things. Why shouldn't you be right over this?'

'Yes, yes.' She could see his pride rising again; he had been somewhat subdued by the fact that she had seen so much more than he.

'We'd better go and find it, then. Don't tell anyone.'

'Don't be so *silly*,' said Josephine impatiently. 'As if I ever should. I've never told anybody but you about Margaret. I couldn't. They'd say "how exciting and how fascinating" and sort of maul her about and she wouldn't be mine any more. That Mrs Ramsey woman must have been a bit like that. No wonder Margaret never appeared again for a time. She wasn't going to be messed about. She's a shy ghost.' She found she could talk about her now, without a pang.

'You're right.'

They turned to leave the room. Simon suddenly laughed.

'To think of Aunt Tessa so keen to find a ghost here and there's been one all the time, *and* one described in a book in her own junk room. I'll bet she's never read it.'

'And if she did there'd be nothing to tell her it was in *her* house. You have to know the Christian name and the story. It just says H——shire. It could be Hampshire. It could be Huntingdonshire. Yet all the same, it's an odd sort of coincidence, the book being here at all. Do you think someone else, perhaps way back, did know? That this is the house that fits that particular story?'

'Could be. And the book has just stayed in the house, through lots of owners perhaps.'

'Oh, if only one knew,' cried Josephine. 'Really I suppose it's more likely that the people before Tessa bought it at a sale. Tessa herself could have bought it at a sale, together with lots of other books, come to that. My father is always buying books at sales and then not reading them very much. It makes my mother very cross.'

'I don't think Aunt Tessa is a very reading sort of person,' said Simon after a moment's reflection. 'She's always out doing something to the animals, or having lots of people in—'

'And doing something to them,' Josephine finished his sentence for him.

'Some people leave people alone. Others don't,' he muttered as if to himself, rather grimly.

'You like to stir people up yourself sometimes,' Josephine

was about to comment, but thought better of it. Suddenly a brilliant idea which excited her very much occurred to her.

'Simon, you know the name of the house has been changed more than once? Tessa was telling my parents about it. Margaret is called Margaret C—— in the book, isn't she? The author just gives the first letter of her surname and no more. Suppose she was Margaret *Christmas*, or perhaps Christian or something near to Christmas as Tessa was saying. The house could have been named after *her*: there were stories about the child ghost many years ago, and they must have gone around the village to get this man hearing of it and then writing about it, so perhaps the name "cold" came then? The village people must have talked about the house a lot, and her rather odd surname and the two just came naturally together, and the grand, proper name of the house became used less and less. Ghosts *make* things cold, I've heard. The temperature drops, or something. Perhaps there were some parts of the house they could never warm. It's nothing to do with clay. It's cold for *ghosts*, Simon.'

'Maybe,' he agreed, a little doubtfully. 'Come on, I want my breakfast. And then we'll look about outside. Aren't you supposed to be going back today sometime?'

'Yes, this morning, but not right away, I don't expect. Mummy and Daddy aren't up yet. And they've got to pack and say goodbye and all the rest of it.'

'My mother comes down from London to lunch here and we go back afterwards,' said Simon. 'Come on, hurry up. We've not much time.'

They ran downstairs together.

# 10

After an hour outside their sense of urgency and eagerness was a little dampened. The snow had practically gone, it was milder and slushy and the birds were beginning to sing a little as if it were spring. The stable yard was thick with mud and they were helped on their explorations by Susie, who trotted about after them with an air of expectancy and eagerness.

'Well, wherever she left it she didn't leave it anywhere around the stables,' Simon said at last. 'Nor in the coalhouse, or where they keep logs.'

'Oh, it must have been found ages ago, if she ever *did* leave it,' said Josephine, beginning to lose faith.

'Well, it wasn't found when that story was written in 1860 or so or the writer would have put it in. He'd have said the valuables were stolen and later recovered or something.'

'The trunk could have been found by somebody who just kept it: a dishonest coachman perhaps.'

'*I* don't think so and I'm going on looking even if you aren't.'

'Oh, I'm going on looking too. It's just that I had such a strong feeling that she'd have dragged it into a little dark shed somewhere near here but there simply doesn't seem to be one.'

'Wait,' said Simon, frowning. 'They must have a gardening shed somewhere. The garages are all new so it's no good looking there but there could be an old gardening shed—only I can't think where it is.'

'There's a new one by the first holly hedge,' said Josephine. 'At least it looks newish to me.'

They went to see, passing Jason on the drive, who was aimlessly kicking a football about. He brightened when he saw them.

'Like a game of something?'

'No. We're busy,' said Simon curtly. 'Come on, Josephine.'

'Sorry!' Josephine called over her shoulder and was amused at Jason's look of surprise to find her and Simon so occupied together. But there was no time for Jason now: it would take up valuable minutes explaining to him.

The shed was obviously new, and contained nothing more than gardening tools and deck chairs.

'There's the boathouse,' said Simon dubiously, looking down the garden.

'She'd never have dragged it down there. Also, do you really think that place, old as it is, has been there since 1790 or whatever? Remember how long ago it was.'

'Yes: it *was* a long time ago,' said Simon, sticking his lower jaw out aggressively. 'But I will *not* be beaten. I'm sure that what we thought happened, did happen.'

'All right then, let's go down and look at that boathouse.'

'All right, we will.'

Without speaking they walked down the garden to the rough ground beneath and to the shore of the lake. The boathouse projected out into the water; it was long and of black timber. It certainly looked quite old.

'She'd have needed a wheelbarrow to get it down here alone,' said Josephine.

'Well, that's not impossible is it? There could easily have been one lying around—'

They climbed up to the boathouse, while the dog splashed in and out of the water. A little to Josephine's surprise she had shown no fear today at coming down to this part of the grounds, so near to the oak avenue.

'Well,' said Simon. 'I dunno.'

Below the boathouse, pulled out of the water onto a concrete base, was a punt. Above this was a kind of timbered shed in which there were poles for the punt, an oar, some coils of rope, a bucket, a wooden box or so, a barrel, a pile of tarpaulins, a spade . . .

'I suppose that couldn't—' said Josephine tentatively. She walked to a corner where behind tarpaulins were several more boxes of various kinds and sizes. She pulled at one; it had a curved top and rusty iron bands across it.

'It couldn't be something like this?' she finished. She had the box right out now: it looked cobwebby and dirty enough, but so very ordinary and undistinguished: not at all what she had been imagining.

'Oh no, surely.' Simon flipped the top open, it was not locked.

Inside was a pile of rotting material.

'It *is*,' said Josephine slowly. 'But—' She was rummaging within the stained and mildewed rags, 'there's nothing here. Nothing heavy. It's just clothes . . . I suppose this could have been a shawl. Ugh!' She held up a long greyish piece of wool which tore and crumbled in her hands as she did so.

'Anybody could have looked through this,' said Simon, 'at any time. It's not particularly hidden. The candlesticks and silver must have all been taken out, if they were ever there. If this really is the right box. It could be any old box.'

He kicked it viciously.

Josephine slid her hand into a piece of rotten silk that had lined the box and been used as a side pocket. It tore away as she did so.

'There's another bit of something in here,' she said.

But Simon had turned away.

Josephine looked at the piece of material. It was badly stained with damp down one side, but at least it held together. She turned it round, could not make it out at first, could not understand it. Why should this be here? Why had Betty put it in? And then she realized that this was the proof she needed. They had been right: this was Betty's box without a doubt and here was Josephine's own personal piece of treasure. She wanted nothing more now.

She folded the piece of material carefully and put it in her pocket.


After a few minutes Josephine realized she was alone in the boathouse, Simon having gone off in disgust. She slammed the lid of the box down, raising a cloud of dust, and shoved it partially back into position. It was much easier to see it now, Miranda and Annabella would probably come across it quite soon if they ever came poking about down here. Well, good luck to them.

'It is Betty's box,' she called, re-emerging in her turn into the weak winter sunlight. 'I suppose by the time it was discovered the material had already rotted and that's why it just got left there.' But she did not tell him what she had found, or why she was so sure it was Betty's box.

'Oh who *cares*,' he grumbled. 'Other people must have

looked into it, lots of them: the secret's all spoiled; there's nothing of value there and I was so sure we were going to find something good.'

The anticlimax of it all was obviously a bitter disappointment and he wandered off, beyond the boathouse where there was a great chalk pit with steep sides slanting down to the lake and shaggy with undergrowth and riddled with rabbit holes. Susie was already racing about here, her nose to the ground.

'There was a rabbit,' said Simon. He wandered along the bottom of the pit, kicking at the lowest holes and making his boots white and slimy.

The dog came nosing about at his feet. She pawed at something, seized it in her mouth and pulled. Then she ran off a little way with a rather naughty expression in her eyes as if she knew she had something she was not allowed.

'What's that then, Susie?' called Simon, cheering up a little.

'Looks like a bone.' Josephine caught up with them. 'Don't let's stay here, it's a depressing sort of place—' she was beginning when Simon wrenched at the bone in the dog's mouth.

'It's a jolly long bone,' he said thoughtfully. 'It's a shin bone I should think, but longer than a sheep—a horse or cow?'

'There's another bone here,' said Josephine, bending down and looking. Simon had kicked at some earth just above a gaping rabbit hole; it was all soft and had fallen in and there were whitish pieces which weren't chalk.

'Wait a moment.' Simon scrabbled with a piece of stone and pulled. A great jagged piece came up.

'My golly,' he said weakly. 'My golly, Josephine, I believe that's part of a human pelvis.'

'Oh no, surely not.'

'It is, it is, I'm nearly sure. We have a skeleton at school in the Biology Lab. I've done all the larger bones, we did them only last term—My golly, Josephine. *This is Betty.*'

'I'm going,' announced Josephine, shivering. 'I simply hate this place.' But she did not stir. 'Even if it is human, I don't see why it should be Betty. It could be somebody else. There could be more than one person lying dead here. It's the right sort of place. There could be bones upon bones.'

'Oh shut up. You're just working yourself up. Look, we know she went off: it was dark, she was in a great state— perhaps she drowned. We know she got *down* to the lake, or we're pretty sure she did.'

'How could she drown on dry land?'

'This is as low as the lake: the water could have come up here at some time in a kind of inlet. Later on perhaps it all dried out. And by then her bones were deep in the mud. I bet she either committed suicide or drowned here by accident.'

'That still doesn't explain why the silver is missing.'

'I've an idea,' cried Simon. 'What if she *was* helped down here by somebody and the somebody knew she had valuable stuff in her box and killed her and then took the things out of the box. They could have hidden the box first. It doesn't matter quite how it happened. But I'll bet that's how it was!'

His eyes sparkled; he was absolutely sure of himself. 'Goodness,' he repeated to himself softly. 'Oh, my goodness. And you know that evening by the lake, before you and Jason came, I told you I heard something in the bushes and a cry! I knew there was something more. This was the *end* of it: it ended here. Golly, Josephine, I'm glad I didn't come round here that night!'

Josephine shivered and was silent. It was certainly an unpleasant place. The steep sides of the pit seemed to close in round them, with greenish saplings leaning over here and there at crazy angles, and everywhere the ghosts of nettles and bramble and brittle-looking elder bushes. It was probably all overgrown here in summer, and so entirely shut off from everything except rabbits. And at last she knew, as far as she could know without proof, how it had been.

Suppose this *was* a human skeleton; the skeleton of Betty (though they had found no skull as yet and she didn't intend to try) and suppose it had happened as Simon had imagined, suppose someone had helped Betty with her box right down to the lakeside and then had helped her to her death, robbed the box of its stolen goods and gone off with them under her shawl?

Yes, under her shawl. Alice! The hard-faced Alice with a mouth like a trap who had led the younger weaker woman astray, who had obviously cared for nobody much: had she become both a murderer and a thief? Had this scene too been enacted, like Joseph's accident, for anybody with eyes to see? If she and Simon had gone beyond the boathouse would they have seen the very end of the story here—one dark figure creeping up behind another, a blow, a cry, a splash, perhaps, and then silence?

The sides of the pit seemed to darken, and close in a little nearer. It smelt of chalky mud and decaying vegetation and of oldness. This place had been an unpleasant place for many years; for centuries, for as long as men had walked on two legs and thought things had spirits.

'I'm getting out of here,' stated Josephine, in as firm a voice as she could summon. A little to her surprise Simon followed her; they scrambled up the side of the pit and began to walk slowly back towards the house, the dog running ahead of them.

'Josephine,' said Simon suddenly, stopping. 'I've thought of something and it scares me. Something about us.'

'What?'

'I think we ought never to meet again. Us together scares me. No, I mean it. Do you realize how much we've found out and seen *together*? How the—the happenings along the avenue got much stronger when you came? How we dreamt together (though I don't think I'd have remembered my dream if you hadn't made me). Then you saw Margaret, and I seemed to start up all the coming and going along the avenue. But us together—you know, I'm really scared.'

'I see what you mean,' said Josephine slowly. 'We sort of increase the power.'

'I'm sure of it. After all, there has to be somebody around who can see things, or nothing would happen at all. Tony and Tessa are quite blind. Someone like Jason's only half and half, and I bet he wouldn't have noticed anything on his own. He kind of got slightly dragged in. I expect years and years have gone by with nothing specially happening to anybody. But if by chance you get two people who are clever and sensitive like us, then wow! It can be dangerous. It was dangerous. We sort of set a pattern going again; that tree falling in much the same place as a tree had fallen before, and a child that would have died. And they did get her doll, Josephine, they did get her doll!'

'Who is they?' asked Josephine helplessly, of him, of the surrounding countryside.

'*I* don't know. Evil spirits, if you like.'

Alice, her mouth like a trap. She loomed dark and high in Josephine's mind, a fearful black shadow, changed to a witch. She had Betty, drunken and writhing, in her grasp. She had Margaret . . .

'It's terrible, being young,' said Josephine suddenly. She saw children, the young and innocent generally, as victims caught and twisted by the evil, groping hands of the world-weary and mature, the stiffening, deadly middle-aged and elderly.

'When I grow up I shan't be like that.' She turned to Simon.

'Like what?'

'Like they are. I shall travel and have beautiful clothes and be happy. I shall do just what I like. I shan't let them do things to me.'

But even as she said it, she wondered. One thought ahead to being grown-up as to a time when all one's problems would be solved; one would always be in control, never be shy and fearful. It was only now, and perhaps also next year that one shrank and shivered. But not after that. Surely?

'I don't know what you're talking about,' cried Simon impatiently, his mind working on quite other lines, making his own drama.

'Now listen. This is very important and serious. I don't think we ever ought to meet again after today. I want you to swear, hold up your hand as I'm doing and repeat after me, using just the same words, except for your name, of course. I'll start first: I, Simon Charles Sinclair, don't *laugh*, this is serious, I, Simon Charles Sinclair do most solemnly swear that if I encounter you (what's your full name, just Josephine?) you, Josephine Palmer by some mischance again, I will have no further speech with you, apart from the necessities of common politeness.'

'Funny to hear *him* talking about politeness,' thought Josephine to herself, but she was impressed, nevertheless, by the solemnity of what they were doing.

'I will shun your company and try to avoid meeting you again, and thereto I plight thee—'

'No you don't,' she cried. 'That's in the marriage service: thereto I plight thee my troth. This is like a sort of *anti*-marriage service!'

'Therefore I solemnly swear to you that I will carry out my bounden promise.'

He continued to hold out his hand, his cheeks flushed, his brow determined, and he was remarkably good-looking; handsome indeed.

'It's a good thing we're not any older than we are,' thought Josephine with a sudden flash of insight. 'Although I still don't really *like* him, there is this bond between us and if I were older ...' and she knew that one day a boy such as Simon might cause her pain. But not now: thank goodness, not yet. She could swear without a pang. And so she held up her hand and began, 'I, Josephine Palmer—' and continued until she had finished.

It was an impressive oath, well worded, and Simon rose in her estimation. A boy with such power over words, such ability to make decisions and to act on them, would get somewhere, parliament perhaps? And though she was not to meet him again in some way the oath reassured her, made a kind of sense of the chaos they were in. She was glad she had shared so much with him, that she was not bearing it all on her own.

Then far away up the hill, at the top of the garden, she saw her father beckoning and waving.

'It must be nearly time for us to go. Simon—don't tell them about finding bones and things until after I've gone. And then pretend you found them on your own. Will you promise?'

'Yes, all right. But I expect I'll have to tell them some-time.'

112

'I know.' And she knew too, without doubt, that he was longing to go back, with plenty of company, to the pit and dig and dig. If there were no candlesticks or silver spoons to be found, bones would do very nicely. There are different kinds of treasure. Or, if one is determined enough, one can make all kinds of things seem to be treasure. Indeed, now they were out of the pit she found that she believed less and less that they were actually Betty's bones they had unearthed, or indeed that they were human bones at all. Yet there remained a basic truth to which they had penetrated and as far as she could be sure of anything she was sure that her vision of Alice robbing and possibly murdering had been correct. Alice, a beast of prey, had ruined poor Betty.

'Shall we say goodbye properly now?' asked Simon. 'Although I'll be coming up to the house with you I shan't be taking any particular notice of you.'

They stopped and faced one another and he took her hand and formally shook it.

There was a pause. They both felt something more was needed.

'Well goodbye, Simon,' she said at last, 'and, and thank you.'

'What are you thanking me for?'

'I don't know, really.' She giggled slightly with embarrassment. There was no putting it into words, but she was thankful for something she had learnt through him about a certain sort of spoilt yet self-sufficient masculinity. And it had been a relief to discover that the wounding contempt with which he had at first seemed to regard her had not been so personally aimed as she had thought. He looked at her a moment and seemed to be searching for the right words.

'You'll be all right at that new school of yours,' he said

at last. 'I should think you might even be quite popular with some people.'

His intention was undoubtedly to be kind and encouraging, and Josephine took it as such.

'Do you really think so?' she said humbly.

It was something: this praise from such as he. And of course he did not know that popularity had been far beyond her aim. Just to pass muster, not to attract unfavourable attention had been all she dared to hope for.

And now, finished with each other, they could easily part.

'Goodbye, Simon.'

'Goodbye.'

A shiver ran down her back, she turned away from him and continued up the slope of the garden towards her father, who waved to her and returned to the house, and as she climbed, she felt she was indeed climbing out of a great dark pit, the air seemed to become softer and softer and lighter and lighter, and the dog began to frisk about and bark and she saw all the other children playing together; the first time they ever had as a group, running in and out round the hedges and up and down the paths. All the garden seemed to be rejoicing.

'Come on, Josephine, come and play with us,' called Miranda, while Jason lay in ambush for her and pounced.

'Oh, do get off Jason, you're tickling.'

'Am I?' he giggled, and tickled harder than ever. As Josephine broke free and ran away laughing until her stomach ached she had a moment's memory of her first day here and how she had been cross, acutely shy and all closed up upon herself. Nevermore could she be quite as she was: a spirit from the past had broken the little icy shell of self, the brittle outer covering with which she was encased, to play its own melody upon her, as upon some musical instrument, and she had responded.

Now Simon had become he, chasing Miranda who screamed with pleasure and excitement. He leapt a flower-bed and caught Rupert, who made for Josephine and Jason who were standing close together. As they scattered Josephine had the strangest sensation for a moment of another body also running, she heard a delighted giggle, and then Rupert caught her. She turned towards Jason, half expecting to find that Annabella had come up between them. But no, Annabella was far away, pedalling her tricycle. It was just that there were so many running, colliding bodies, perhaps. She had Jason now by the sleeve of his jersey, he was not a very fast runner. But he was a nice person, she liked him immensely. She liked them all. What a pity it was time to go home. But life was so often like that; just as one began to relax and enjoy oneself, the party was over.

'Josephine!' her mother appeared at the front door. 'We're off in a minute.'

Inside the hall, at the bottom of the stairs, was her parents' big suitcase. Her mother and father, Jason's father and Tony and Tessa Swift were all gathered together, talking hard. Josephine noticed a difference in them; they had suddenly become less polite and more truly friendly, as if they knew each other a good deal better. In some way this seemed to be due to the fact that her father had at last apparently told the Swifts that he was out of work.

'But it's the simplest thing in the world, Don,' Tessa Swift was saying. 'Daddy has his finger in so many pies. As soon as he's back from the Bahamas which should be within the next week or so I'll telephone him. I'm sure there'll be no difficulty.'

'Come on darling, we're just waiting for you and your suitcase,' said her mother briskly. 'You have packed it, I suppose?'

'Oh goodness! Nearly packed,' cried Josephine, running up the stairs two at a time.

Of course she had completely forgotten her suitcase, forgotten to pack at all. But it would not take long.

'Don't forget your toothbrush!' called her mother after her. 'And don't be too long over it.'

Her room, now comfortable and familiar, awaited her. It seemed a long time ago since she had first greeted it with such dismay. Her belongings were strewn about it in a homely sort of way, the window was open and it was not particularly cold. She put her suitcase upon the unmade bed and began to fling garments into it. Her books, comics, toothbrush, hairbrush, slippers, underclothes—what else now? An afterthought caused her to retrieve her pyjamas from underneath the pillow. A dirty pair of socks all over fluff from under the bed. Anything else down there? Goodness, her diary. Wouldn't do to leave that behind. Though she had finished it off far too early, there was in fact nothing she wanted to add. She flicked the pages thoughtfully over to the last one of all where she saw the large letters slantwise across the end of the year where she had put 'Nothing more has happened.' A picture would kind of round matters off, so without thinking of anything particularly she hastily drew a bird, which turned into an eagle with huge beak and wingspread bearing something—a rabbit—a baby perhaps?—in its talons. A good nasty picture to round off the diary satisfactorily.

A floorboard at the door creaked and she turned round hastily, expecting—what? But it was only Simon standing looking in at her. He had a piece of paper in his hand.

'My address,' he said rapidly. 'And will you give me yours? It's just struck me that there's no reason why we shouldn't write to one another, if we either of us ever see anything again. It would be nice to tell somebody who understands.'

'Yes, that's a good idea.' She told him her address and put his slip of paper into her diary. She didn't expect to write to him ever, but one never knew. The bird she had drawn caught her attention again and she was just sketching in some tail feathers when her mother appeared. Simon hesitated a moment, then went and she did not see him again.

'Really Josephine, I didn't tell you to go upstairs and draw pictures,' her mother said. 'Is your suitcase ready?'

'Absolutely ready.' Josephine scrawled very rapidly under the bird, 'Simon and I swore never to meet again,' was sure he would have liked her to record this, then threw in her diary and snapped the case shut. There was nothing more to wait for, the visit was over. She followed her mother out of the room; a nothing room now, not hers, not anybody's.

A minute later she was outside the house, standing on the gravelled drive by their car while they said the last farewells.

'Goodbye, thank you very much indeed for having me, I have enjoyed it,' said Josephine rapidly, actually managing to look her hostess in the face while saying these words: then paused, because was 'enjoy' the right word for her experiences at Cold Christmas? She must try and say something else to Tessa who was looking a little drooped as if each person's going diminished her, for whom in some quite unexplainable way she felt a little sorry, and who had tried so hard and missed so much.

'I think you'll find it warmer in the house now,' was

what she ended by saying. It had come out a bit wrong and of course Tessa didn't quite understand.

'Warmer?' she cried vaguely. 'Yes, it is warmer. Much warmer! Goodbye Josephine, my dear. I'll be seeing you again I'm sure, but I do want to say another very special thank you for rescuing Annabella like that. Oh, I do wish you weren't going. And Bill and Jason too. They'll be bearing Tony off with them, so I'll be quite bereft.'

'Must start film-making again sometime, you know,' said her husband, looking jaunty.

'Oh, he's never so happy as when he's away from me!' she cried, laughing brightly to show it was a joke.

'Goodbye!'

'Goodbye!'

Josephine and her parents got into their car and it moved slowly off down the drive. They rounded a corner and had a short way to go between fields bordered by iron railings before they were out on the road.

'Fancy Tessa's father being the chairman of so many companies,' said Mrs Palmer after a moment's pause. 'Oh Don. I do believe he really will be a help to you.'

'Hmn, we'll see,' was all her husband's rejoinder. 'We'll see "when Daddy comes back from the Bahamas",' he added in a not very good imitation of Tessa's voice.

'Now Don, you're to be nice about Tessa,' said Mrs Palmer, laughing a little despite herself.

'You mistake me. I like her very much. I didn't exactly enjoy the holiday and you know I didn't take to him particularly, but I think she is a very nice person and I don't mean to laugh at her seriously, you know.'

'I'm sure the break did you a lot of good, even if nothing else comes out of it, and Josephine too. You see, you made friends with those boys after all, didn't you? I thought you would.'

But Josephine was no longer listening. Sitting in the back of the car by herself, she had slipped the little piece of material out of her trouser pocket where she had put it for safe keeping, and she looked at it again.

And this is what she saw. A greenish piece of stuff, discoloured in places by age and damp, with marks where it had been previously folded. Unevenly worked in a white cross-stitch over this background were the words: 'The Lord is my Shepherd, I shall not Want,' and beneath them a whitish splodge with four legs which must have been meant for a lamb. At the bottom was worked in a much smaller but still uneven stitch: 'This Samplar sewn by Margaret Christ—' and the last three letters were quite obliterated by damp. The date underneath said 179—and again the last number was impossible to read.

This was part of Betty's treasure too, and it had remained, when other more valuable things had gone, vanished without trace into the mists of time.

Margaret Christmas. She could not sew very well. She had wanted to play with the stable lad and ride on the cart horse. She had wanted so very much the company of other children.

'Look, Josephine, look at the donkeys,' exclaimed her mother. 'They're trying to race us.'

The whole pack of donkeys, led by the venerable yet still lusty Albert, the grandfather of them all, were cantering along beside the railings as if they were trying to catch up with the car and speak to the people within. What did they want to say? They were hee-hawing and kicking out with their back legs and frisking about in a great state of excitement.

And then Josephine knew what it was, for on Albert's back she saw, for an instant of time, a child seated, a child with black hair streaming behind her, and she was laughing and waving and bouncing up and down. Did she call out triumphantly, 'At last! At last!' Or was it the echo of a donkey's cry 'Ah-har! Ah-har!' Oh, why did donkeys cry out so strangely? What did they know? What did animals know?

And then she wasn't there. Albert gave one gigantic buck and stopped dead. The donkeys behind him changed from a canter, to a trot, to a walk. Some of them were beginning to graze.

'Goodbye, goodbye!' cried Josephine at the top of her voice, leaning far out of the window. 'I shall always remember you. I'm glad you got a ride at last!'

'No, you didn't get a ride on a donkey, did you?' remarked her father, mishearing and misunderstanding her. 'Bad luck. Perhaps some other time.'

'There won't be another time,' said Josephine, as he turned the car out of the drive onto the road beyond.

A little rain spattered against the window; rain to melt away the last traces of ice, to cleanse and obliterate.

'And now for home,' said Mrs Palmer, settling herself comfortably.

And so they drove out of Cold Christmas, back into the ordinary world.

*Also by Nina Beachcroft*

## UNDER THE ENCHANTER

*The boy is in nice and deep. A most satisfactory little piece of enchantment.*

Laura was right to mistrust Mr Strange. Ever since he lured Andrew and her down to the lake, Andrew has been behaving oddly. What happened at the lake? Was it a dream? Was it a kind of hypnotism? As Laura watches her brother, she is forced to believe it is deadly enchantment. But only Laura can see the change in him, and only she can save him : . .

'This beautifully written book is filled with ancient magic, utterly remote from pretty fairy tales, it is often chilling and always enchanting . . . I defy any reader of whatever age to put it down before the end.'

*Books and Bookmen*

Nina Beachcroft

## *WELL MET BY WITCHLIGHT*

*'Well met by witchlight' she found herself suddenly saying out loud. She could not be sleeping on such a night. It was a night for magic if ever a night was.*

Mary is no ordinary witch. Her powers have lain dormant for many years.

Can she triumph over the evil black witch? The malice, cruelty and uncanny evil of that face held them rooted; it was worse than they could have conceived possible . . .

# A Selected List of Fiction from Mammoth

While every effort is made to keep prices low, it is sometimes necessary to increase prices at short notice. Mammoth Books reserves the right to show new retail prices on covers which may differ from those previously advertised in the text or elsewhere.

The prices shown below were correct at the time of going to press.

All these books are available at your bookshop or newsagent, or can be ordered direct from the publisher. Just tick the titles you want and fill in the form below.

**Mandarin Paperbacks**, Cash Sales Department, PO Box 11, Falmouth, Cornwall TR10 9EN.

Please send cheque or postal order, no currency, for purchase price quoted and allow the following for postage and packing:

UK 80p for the first book, 20p for each additional book ordered to a maximum charge of £2.00.

BFPO 80p for the first book, 20p for each additional book.

Overseas including Eire £1.50 for the first book, £1.00 for the second and 30p for each additional book thereafter.

NAME (Block letters) ........................................................................................................

ADDRESS ........................................................................................................................

........................................................................................................................

........................................................................................................................